Wide Open Spaces

By

Cadee Brystal

Wide Open Spaces

By Cadee Brystal

ISBN-10: 0991441702
ISBN-13: 978-0-9914417-0-9

This is a work of fiction. Names, characters and
incidents are either the product of the
author's imagination or are used fictitiously.
Any resemblance to actual events or persons,
living or dead, is coincidental.

CHRISTIAN BOOKS IN MULTIPLE GENRES, JOIN CHRISTIAN INDIE
AUTHOR ~ READERS GROUP ON FACEBOOK. OPPORTUNITIES TO
LEARN MORE GREAT CHRISTIAN AUTHORS.
HTTPS://WWW.FACEBOOK.COM/GROUPS/291215317668431/

Dear Reader,

I'm excited to welcome you to Miller's Bend, a friendly small town on the plains of South Dakota. The characters you'll meet are not Texas Rangers or former Navy Seals – they are just regular people who, like you, live, laugh, love, and do the best they can to leave the world a bit better than they found it. They are imperfect, struggle from time to time, and sometimes they make mistakes. They are human – not superhuman.

I hope you will embrace them and let Riley and Shelby into your literary hearts. Their story is sweet, but also has an element of suspense as they receive Christian guidance from the kindly Mrs. Holmes, as they go about learning the Lessons of Love in Miller's Bend.

If you enjoy Shelby and Riley's romance, be sure to look for my next book, *Breaking Free*. It features Riley's brother, Andrew, and Shelby's friend, Allison, as each tries to move past their respective histories and forge together into a new and happier future.

Happy reading!
Cadee Brystal

THANK YOU

Thank you to my parents who so highly stressed education in our household. Thanks to my family members who kept saying, "You should write," and to my daughters who would at times have to wait while I finished a paragraph, page or chapter, before I would turn my attention to them.

Thanks to my volunteer collaborators, Terri, Jessica, Marlys, Makayla, Tammie, Char and Jenny; and to my husband who never once called me crazy … in respect to my writing.

I love you all!

"GOOD THINGS COME
TO THOSE WHO WAIT."

One of Cadee's high school teachers had counseled her, saying, "If you want to write, then write." But she had known that real life would call for a real job, and enrolled in a state university where she earned degrees in an agricultural field, animal science and journalism.

And then life happened. While employed by a weekly newspaper in a South Dakota town not unlike the fictional Miller's Bend, she met the man she would marry. They have been married more than 20 years and have been blessed with two daughters.

Cadee's love of the written word was rekindled and she began to write in the early morning hours, before the household members awakened. In a matter of months, the characters of Riley, Shelby, and their friends and families, had taken on lives of their own.

Cadee has maintained the importance of developing compelling characters who live out their stories on the pages of clean, enjoyable books, while delivering a message of Christian faith applicable in our contemporary lives.

CONTENTS

Chapter One   1

Chapter Two   13

Chapter Three   21

Chapter Four   29

Chapter Five   37

Chapter Six   47

Chapter Seven   53

Chapter Eight   65

Chapter Nine   73

Chapter Ten   81

Chapter Eleven   89

Chapter Twelve   95

Chapter Thirteen   101

Chapter Fourteen   107

Chapter Fifteen   113

Chapter Sixteen   123

Chapter Seventeen   133

Chapter Eighteen   141

Chapter Nineteen   151

Chapter Twenty   161

Chapter Twenty-one   177

Chapter Twenty-two   189

Chapter Twenty-three   199

Chapter Twenty-four   209

Chapter Twenty-five   217

Chapter Twenty-six   227

Chapter Twenty-seven   237

CHAPTER ONE

Some folks have common sense; some folks have book sense, and some poor souls don't have either.

He definitely belonged in the last category. It wasn't kind, but as the rotund speaker rambled on, the thought had sprung into Shelby's consciousness. Her mother's words echoed in Shelby's mind: *some poor souls don't have either. And,* Shelby added mentally, *they shouldn't pick up a microphone if they are in that third classification.*

Shelby Sweetin was covering the first big story in her fledgling career as a news reporter for the Miller's Bend Chronicle and firmly reminded herself to keep her mind focused on the proceedings before her. It would be death to her career if she misquoted an important local official. Shelby tried to make sense of the speaker's comments as she rushed to record his words in her reporter's notebook. Since graduating from the university in May, she had moved to the small town in South Dakota and had begun her newswriting career. So far, she had written accounts of the mundane: weddings, social news, weather and crop stories, as well as reporting the routine meetings and community events. She longed to show the world, or at least the residents of Miller's Bend, what she could do if given a good story – one with some meat to it. But no important stories had been entrusted to her, until tonight.

"There's no sense in it!" the speaker yelled as his jowls shook and his face flushed. Dark sweat stains formed on his worn, dirty T-shirt and were expanding at an alarming rate. The effect gave the speaker a nasty look, and Shelby suspected a nasty aroma as well. "You're up to something sneaky," he shot toward the members of the school board who were assembled on stage. Some board members looked at their laps, some looked into the audience and some watched the speaker move restlessly as he ranted. "You decided to do this and now you are trying to shove it down our throats and we don't want any part of it!"

"That old football field was good enough for generations of Cougars and it'll be good enough for kids these days, too!" the speaker bellowed. He had built up a head of steam and Shelby was beginning to fear that he might have a stroke or a heart attack. "There ain't no reason to go diggin' it out and puttin' in a new field," he fairly yelled into the microphone. The man was beginning to pant from the exertion of trying to make his point and his face glowed with a furious shade of red. "Times is hard and there ain't 'nuff money to build this complex thing," he shouted. "We won't be paying any more taxes for this!" Several of the 50 or so people gathered at the open meeting of the Miller's Bend School Board winced and clapped their hands over their ears as the sound system squealed as if to accentuate his statement.

General commotion reigned as the school's IT man ran for the controls intent on cutting the power to the speakers. The superintendent moved quickly and efficiently to the speaker's side and addressed him quietly while the microphone was dead. Shelby strained to try to catch bits of the conversation, but couldn't pick out anything. Chairs squeaked and people murmured as they took advantage of the brief break, shifting and resettling into more comfortable positions. Some grabbed their coats and left, while others spoke quietly to their neighbors about the building project and the information presented by various speakers during the first of what promised to be numerous public meetings.

Needing to learn the identity of the speaker for the story she would write as soon as the meeting concluded, Shelby looked around for a friendly face, someone who wouldn't think she was foolish for not knowing. Twisting in her seat, her gaze bounced from face to face. She glanced around seeing business owners, parents, men and women, people whose clothing and stances, as well as their expressions, told Shelby that the crowd was a diverse bunch coming from various backgrounds. They were all gathered here tonight by a common concern or interest in the proposed building project that would cost the Miller's Bend School District in excess of $1.25 million.

This was definitely big news in the small town!

Shelby considered waiting until after the meeting to find out who the speaker was. She glanced around once more, and then she leaned toward Marjorie Fields, a kind older woman who had proven to be friendly and helpful since Shelby's arrival in the close-knit community. "Marjorie. Hi, Marjorie," Shelby said in a low tone, adding a smile and friendly wave. Shelby's eyes continued to roam the faces once more. "Can you tell me what his name is?" Shelby whispered quickly.

Marjorie had smiled and leaned toward Shelby as well, bridging a portion of the space between them. "Who?" She paused and followed Shelby's gaze before answering, "Oh, you mean Riley?" came the louder than necessary response. *Riley? Could that be right? He's too old to be a Riley.* Shelby realized her attention had traveled to a group of younger men standing near the side of the meeting room. Mentally chastising herself for checking out the scenery, rather than focusing on her assignment, Shelby pulled her gaze to Marjorie's eyes. She blinked and shook her head as if to clear her thinking. With her pen poised over her notebook, Shelby asked, "Riley what? I need his last name, too."

Marjorie's brow creased. "Now why would you need Riley's name?" she wondered aloud. "That Wheeler boy has just been hanging along the wall with his posse of troublemakers all night," she added. Shelby's curious look faded as she unconsciously returned her gaze to the group of three men who looked to be about her own age. The three men were as different as could be: one tall and lean with blond hair that curled in an unruly fashion; one short and broad with long hair which was extremely dark, and then there was the one who fit in the middle – neither tall nor short, brown hair, medium build. Nothing remarkable, nothing to make him stand out in a crowd. Except, perhaps his expression which was warm and friendly, almost playful.

She felt the heat of a deep blush burn her cheeks as the middle one slowly turned his face toward her and with a very deliberate look he winked! Shelby was horrified as she realized that the man, whom she had never even met, was flirting with her.

4

She quickly turned her head away from "the posse". As she did, three things happened simultaneously – she became aware of the speculative gleam in sweet old Mrs. Fields' eye; her brain registered the deep rumble as the trio of men laughed, and, worst of all, somehow her blush deepened further. How humiliating! Too embarrassed to look around, she dropped her eyes to the notes she had been taking during the community meeting. She hoped she had been discreet in pulling the pony tail band from her hair as she let it fall to form a screen against the eyes that had been studying her.

Brilliant, Shelby, just brilliant! Some reporter you're going to be! Shelby had known for years just how easily and quickly her body would betray her by presenting the crimson flush anytime she felt … well, pretty much any emotion. Surprise, embarrassment, pleasure, awkwardness and others would easily cause a deep crimson blush on her otherwise flawless complexion. Yep, good old Shelby would blush like a summer rose. Not a dainty little pinkness in the cheeks either, she would get as red as a beet and sustain it for several minutes.

Thankfully, the disturbance of the squealing microphone, coupled with whatever the superintendent had said privately, had caused the bumbling speaker to give up and return to his seat. The school district superintendent reclaimed center stage and looked as though he was about to launch the next phase of the offensive. "Now Steven, we don't want anyone to get too worked up at this point," Arthur Jones purred in a placating manner. "The school board has put a tremendous amount of time and effort into researching options. And I am compelled to assure you that every single member of the board is in agreement that we have chosen the best course of action for the citizens." The man made a broad sweeping gesture to include the entire membership of the board in his statement.

"You, the citizens, have duly elected these fine people to represent your positions in the operation of the school and we understand that you have placed your trust in us to do so," Arthur continued. The mesmerizing tone seemed to lull some audience members into a trance. Shelby sensed a general settling among those present. While Steven No-name had been disorganized in his delivery, there had been several audience members whose body language indicated they agreed with at least part of what Steven had tried in his bumbling, ineffective way to express.

Shelby kept her eyes either on her notebook or on the various speakers for the remainder of the meeting. She didn't dare glance toward either the posse or Mrs. Fields for fear of further embarrassment. At the conclusion of the meeting, Shelby snatched up her coat and bag and moved quickly toward the front of the room where Arthur was explaining the board's position to a few of the citizens who had moved in to surround him. Shelby needed to learn the identity of Steven No-name, and there was no way she would approach Mrs. Fields again this day.

Intent on moving forward toward the front of the room, Shelby worked against the tide of people who were hustling to leave. They were rushing to get to their homes, their kids, their lives. She had no one – nothing – to hurry home to, but she still felt an urgency to escape the meeting room. Just as soon as she had Steven's name she could go. Shelby's mind registered that something was off just as a shiver tripped up her spine. But before she could look around for the cause, a hand closed over her upper arm. Shelby whirled around and stepped back, away from whoever had grabbed her. "You!" she gasped.

Riley Wheeler was astounded at the fury he saw in the flashing blue eyes of this slight woman. No, he noted, her expression was tainted with another emotion – fear. He quickly dropped the hold he had on her arm and slid his hand to the back of his own neck. Riley smoothly flashed the smile that had helped him get out of tight spots since he had learned to use it in grade school. He'd developed the habit of irritating Mrs. Johnson back then, and had adapted the endearing smile to help soften the punishments she would dole out.

With a relaxed stance and smile in place, Riley began the delivery intended to cool the anger he saw burning in the little blonde from the newspaper, and lessen her trepidation. "Easy, now," his voice rumbled softly as it reached Shelby's ears. She stiffened, not appreciating the patronizing tone she had picked up in his words. Sensing her defensive response, Riley tried again, "Aw' shucks, Missy, I didn't mean any harm …"

He inhaled deeply preparing to add to his statement, but she cut him off abruptly. "Don't you 'aw shucks, Missy' me!" she demanded. At his startled and confused expression she exclaimed in a jagged whisper "I don't take you for a down-home plowboy, and I'm not Missy."

The little spitfire had him nailed. Huh, who knew she would be able to head him off at the pass? He smiled as he thought how much fun she might be if he could encourage her to put her hackles down. "Now, just hold on," Riley began carefully. She held her tongue, but she held her ground, too. She even advanced on Riley a bit. And she waited. Her face was heart shaped with those unbelievably blue eyes, light freckling across her cheeks, and her shimmering blond hair still hung loose. Absently Riley wondered why she had let her hair loose from its pony tail holder – had it been a conscious act to hide her blush from the crowd? Or had she simply moved to hide from him?

She began to turn away and Riley instinctively reached out toward her again, but stopped himself. That one brief touch had shocked him, but also apparently had spiked her anger and he was hesitant to push her farther. "Wait." Riley said quietly. Then, when she didn't appear to notice, he added in a hoarse whisper to himself, "Please?"

Shelby had begun moving toward the front of the room again on her mission to reach Jones and finish getting the information she needed. Maybe he would even give her an honest quote, instead of the sugar-glazed verbal confectionery that he had been delivering to those gathered with mesmerizing eloquence. She froze when she thought she heard a whispered plea from the brash Riley. She couldn't have heard correctly. The man was so blatantly cocky – first winking at her, then grabbing her by the arm – but now he sounded genuine. *"Wait. Please?"* Shelby couldn't simply ignore him.

Shelby turned slowly. Her eyes locked on his and she waited. The room had nearly cleared, but she wasn't aware of anything but the piercing look in Riley's eyes. She had thought those eyes were brown – just a plain old, run of the mill brown – but now as they held her in place, she studied them. The rich color reminded her of caramel, and there were extra flecks of color that seemed to make his eyes dance. Shelby gave herself a mental shake. She needed to clear this up and get back to work.

Each of them took a hesitant step toward the other. And paused expectantly. Suddenly, Shelby's mother's advice was sounding in her head again, this time reminding her that a soft answer turns away wrath: but grievous words stir up anger. She knew what had to be done – she had to apologize for overreacting. Shelby lowered her eyes and tried to relax her muscles. Looking up again she glimpsed emotions in Riley's eyes – kindness, vulnerability, uncertainty and something else, a sort of longing. Whatever it was that she saw, it took her breath away. "I'm sorry," Riley said ever so quietly, only for her ears.

"I appreciate it, but I'm afraid that I am the one at fault here," Shelby answered gently. "I reacted badly because I was embarrassed. I should be apologizing to you." Reality seemed to be suspended for a moment while they regarded each other, until a man bumped Shelby's shoulder as he rushed from the front of the room toward the exit. Jostled back to the present, Shelby looked away, then back to Riley. "I'm sorry, but I need to catch Mr. Jones before he gets away," she explained as she glanced over her shoulder. "Maybe we could start over sometime?"

"Uh, yeah," Riley paused, unsure of where to go from here or what to suggest. "I guess I'll be seeing you around town." He started to turn away and then swiveled back to face Shelby once more. The intensity in his gaze was even stronger now. "When I came over here... I mean ..." He had to clear his throat before he continued, "When I grabbed your arm, I just needed to stop you and tell you that I'm sorry if I flustered you earlier. I hope I didn't upset you."

Then he turned and was gone. The remaining school board members were at the door now. Shelby had missed her chance to talk with them. She looked to Mr. Jones and smiled as she moved swiftly toward him. "Mr. Jones, can I ask you to clarify a few points?"

Arthur Jones glared at her disapprovingly. He waited until the others had filed out of the building and let the tension in Shelby build. The man was a master at controlling situations and controlling people. Shelby grew nervous under his scrutiny and shifted her bag. "It will only take a few minutes," she offered.

His expression turned even darker, "We are talking about a project that will be a $1.25 million investment and you think you can get the story in 'a few minutes'?" he scoffed. "I'm very disappointed in Catherine. She should have known to cover this herself instead of sending a wet-behind-the-ears wannabe reporter."

Shelby felt the verbal slap to her core. She wanted to be taken seriously, to prove herself. She was a responsible person, yet earlier tonight she had embarrassed herself on a personal level, and now she had done it professionally as well. "I'm sorry, Mr. Jones," she said, trying to recover from her misstep. "I didn't want to hold you up longer than necessary, I'm sure you want to get home to your family." Shelby straightened her stance and looked him in the eye. "I am more than happy to spend whatever time is needed to do this story properly."

Jones had switched off the lights while Shelby had tried to sway him, and he was now standing outside the door, holding it open, waiting impatiently for her to exit. He slowly shook his head before responding, "Well, young lady, I'd have thought you would want to interview me tonight, but I guess you had more important business to attend. I'm locking the building now – you want to be locked in or locked out?"

Cadee Brystal

CHAPTER TWO

Locked out. Shelby was most definitely locked out – and in more ways than one. She had left the meeting last night, having missed her chance to speak with Miller's Bend School Superintendent Arthur Jones. Shelby had offered all the interview options she could think of, begging him to meet with her today, as she dogged him while he moved to his Ford Excursion after locking the main doors of the school.

He had slid into the driver's seat, inserted the key in the ignition, then looked Shelby straight in the eye and said, "Honey, you had your chance and you were off flirting with that troublemaker, Riley Wheeler. You really need to learn who's who and what's what or you may as well go running home to your Mama and Papa." Then he had purposefully slammed the door on the vehicle, and on the conversation. He left her standing in the darkened parking lot staring after him as he drove away.

It didn't appear that the man had a forgiving bone in his body as he had steadfastly refused to meet with her today. She'd been phoning his office since 7:45 a.m. and it would appear that he was ignoring her with ease.

Locked out. Shelby pondered just how "locked out" she was. She'd been evicted from the school. Mr. Jones was locking her out today. She had even been locked out of her own home last night.

When Shelby had arrived at her one-bedroom utility apartment after the meeting, she was dumbstruck as she discovered that she had locked herself out of her own home. Since her place was a renovated basement, her landlord lived upstairs. She swallowed what was left of her pride and knocked on the main floor entrance. After a moment the door inched open revealing the frailest looking little old lady that Shelby had ever known. MaryAnn Holmes, with her bluish-gray hair and glassy silver-gray eyes, was almost ghost-like. She could easily have been one of the soulless undead in one of the popular lines of literature that Shelby's youngest sister, Suzanna, enjoyed reading.

But, Shelby had learned early on in the application process for the apartment, Mrs. Holmes' looks were deceiving. The woman's spirit was lively and her mind quick and sharp. Mrs. Holmes had rules and some very high standards for her renters. Pets were acceptable; overnight male guests were not acceptable; drugs were not acceptable; alcohol was not acceptable. The same was true for swearing and "raucous" music. "And we will go to church together every Sunday morning and you will accompany me to Bible Study or services Wednesday evenings," Mrs. Holmes had concluded.

The conditions of being a renter in the Holmes home were surprising, but Shelby wasn't offended and had agreed. At least she would get to know people and pick up some tips for stories, Shelby had thought. She would also find a church home in her new community.

As Shelby stood on the lighted stoop buffeted by the late fall winds, she was glad to have Mrs. Holmes as a friend of sorts. "Good evening Mrs. Holmes, I'm so sorry to bother you. I hope I didn't wake you," Shelby paused, but continued rubbing her hands together in a subconscious attempt to warm them. A cold front had moved in during the day, dropping the temperatures. Dried leaves skittered across the street and the wind whistled an eerie tune in the branches above.

"My goodness, child, what's the matter?" the kind older woman's eyes had gone from reflecting curiosity to showing concern as she opened the door wider. "Come in, come in. You'll catch your death standing out there in the cold." Securing the door against an uncharacteristically wintery blast that had fairly shoved Shelby into the house, Mrs. Holmes turned again to the young woman who looked far more lost that she was letting on.

"I've locked myself out of the apartment," Shelby confided. "Do you have an extra key I can use?"

The older lady didn't seem to hear, or at least offered no comment on the situation with the locked door, but turned her attention to making Shelby feel comfortable and welcome. "Come and sit on the sofa, dear. Pull the afghan over your shoulders to help warm up and I'll whip up some nice tea for us. Then we will have that little chat that you need," Mrs. Holmes said as she flew into action. Shelby had barely settled on the sofa when her hostess returned bearing a silver tray with a China teapot and two cups and saucers. To Shelby's amazement, there was also a plate of her favorite cookies.

"I swear ... she must be an angel," Shelby said a whispered thanks as the tray was settled on the antique coffee table. Then in a louder voice she addressed her kind neighbor, "Thank you, Mrs. Holmes. I didn't mean for you to go to any trouble. Do you have a bedtime snack like this every night?"

"Oh, no," she laughed. "My dear, I would be the size of a house if I ate cookies every time I desire one. I just had a feeling this afternoon, that cookies would be in order tonight. I can't really explain it, but I've learned to trust my feelings," the elder lady smiled. "So I had a baking day. There's plenty to share – I have some wrapped for you to take home and some for you to take to work tomorrow."

"And so you know the next time you mutter under your breath, I do hear very well, dear," Mrs. Holmes changed the subject from sweets to seriousness. "I am not an angel and do not wish to be one for several more years, if you get my drift," she added, raising a silvery-gray eyebrow expressively.

Shelby's cheeks began to heat and her eyes were getting watery. "There, there, dear," the elderly lady said as she handed a cup and saucer to Shelby. "It's alright; I just thought you should know where you stand with me. And likewise I should know where I stand with you."

The pair sipped their tea and enjoyed the frosted sugar cookies that had been laid out before them. They spoke of the weather – how it had turned from Indian summer to a cold and windy precursor to what was doomed to be a record-breaking winter. They spoke about topics from the TV news which was broadcast quietly in the other corner of the immaculate living room.

As each woman enjoyed the presence and companionship of the other, Shelby's respect for Mrs. Holmes grew and deepened. Shelby began to feel more settled and certain of herself. She felt that she was wrapped in a kind of warmth. It was a warmth that felt profound. As Shelby began to realize what she felt, Mrs. Holmes cleared her throat, as though to draw her guest's attention.

"God brought you to my door tonight instead of your own and I have a feeling He had been putting the steps in place all day long, so why don't you tell me what's going on," Mrs. Holmes said. The kindness and love radiating from Mrs. Holmes' countenance really did inspire a person to want to tell all their trials and tribulations. Shelby knew instinctively that, whether Mrs. Holmes' admitted to it, she was indeed Shelby's angel.

Shelby told the sweet grandmotherly soul the events of the evening. She spilled the whole story including her failures, confusion and frustrations. Shelby confessed that she wanted to establish herself as a real reporter, one who covered important news. She wanted to make a name for herself and to be respected for her work. With two older siblings and two younger ones, Shelby had often felt obscure, or even invisible, in the family. She admitted to Mrs. Holmes how she had longed to stand out and be noticed.

"I'm so glad that you've entrusted me with your feelings," Mrs. Holmes had said quietly, when Shelby had finished. "You know you are lucky to have grown up nestled in the heart of your family. I think from what you've shared, that you may have set your sights on a goal that is inconsequential," she said.

"The people who love you do so because of who you are, not because of who you want to be. The same is true of respect," the older woman continued. "You will be respected for who you truly are inside."

"Interviewing people who believe themselves to be important is not what will make your work be important. That's not what will make you feel whole and content," she advised. "And be careful that in your zest to prove yourself, you do not just become a tool that the powerful people use to get what they want."

Shelby frowned as she considered Mrs. Holmes advice. Would interviewing Mr. Jones lead her to be respected, or would people view her as being a mouthpiece for his point of view? "I'll be careful in my reporting, Mrs. Holmes," Shelby said at length, "Thank you for … everything."

"Child, I know life can seem overwhelming, but you need to remember what is important," the elder advised. She kindly wrapped an arm around Shelby's shoulder. "You are trying to prove yourself to a lot of audiences, and the only one that matters is God."

"Somewhere in the Bible it tells us that we need God as our partner. One of the authors said 'Come to me, all who labor and are heavy laden, and I will give you rest. Take my yoke upon you, and learn from me, for I am gentle and lowly in heart, and you will find rest for your souls,'" Mrs. Holmes advised.

The truth of the verse hit Shelby. She had been trying to prove herself to her co-workers, her family, community members and to the "important people", like Mr. Jones. But it was her own image of who she was trying to become, that she wanted to portray. What was the image that God wanted her to portray? It would take some time and prayer to find the answer. "I think it was Matthew," Shelby commented idly.

"Pardon?" Mrs. Holmes asked.

"Matthew. I believe it was Matthew who wrote the passage. I will check and let you know," Shelby answered. "You have been wonderful to me tonight. Thank you so much for helping me. And thank you for listening to my ranting."

"My dear, when God brings a wandering youngster to my door, I can do no less than invite him or her into my home and into His family," the waif of a woman replied tenderly. "And I'm pleased to learn that you've had some Bible teachings."

Cadee Brystal

CHAPTER THREE

"… locked out." Shelby became aware, ever so slowly, that someone was addressing her. As she came out of her reverie, Shelby cast her glance slowly upward and to her right. There stood her mentor of sorts, Bobbie, who had been a dedicated employee of The Chronicle for nearly twenty years.

"What did you say?" Shelby asked. She was, once again embarrassed by her own unprofessional behavior. She felt her cheeks beginning to heat with a blush since she had been caught daydreaming at her workstation. "I'm sorry, Bobbie."

Bobbie only smiled, then with extreme patience said, "I was saying that it looks like that old computer has you locked out. Again." She pointed to the monitor which flashed a message of doom. "I think I'll have to talk Charlie into getting you a new machine. From there, he can convince the boss."

Bobbie stepped back, "Well?" she said.

"Well, what?" Shelby countered, feeling that she had not quite caught up yet.

"Well, you had better get going!" Bobbie paused and narrowed her eyes in the way that all mothers do when they are seeing right through a child. "You didn't hear any of what I said, did you?"

Clearly there was no point in trying to fib to her co-worker. "No, I was deep in thought and didn't even know you were there. Sorry. What is it?" Shelby asked as a fist of dread began to constrict her stomach. What had she missed? It looked as though it had been something vital.

"I'll scold you later," Bobbie smiled as she said the words, easing some of Shelby's tension. "Mr. Arthur Jones returned your *tenth* phone call – I think that's what he said," Bobbie looked as though she needed to ponder that. Then she added in a rush, "He said he will answer *three* questions for your story *if* you are in his office within ten minutes," Bobbie grinned broadly. "I'm proud of you, you've cracked the old man with the heart of granite," she added as a sidebar. *Proud of me?* Shelby was overwhelmed that her senior coworker could be proud of her.

"Better hurry though – that was five minutes ago!" Bobbie chuckled at Shelby's panicked expression. She was already scrambling to grab her notebook, pen and car keys, when Bobbie added, "Don't waste any of those questions with something stupid like, 'How are you, today?' The old coot would count that as one of the three!" Bobbie was laughing. As Shelby hit the door she heard Bobbie turn her attention to Charlie, the boss' husband, "We need to get that girl a new computer. She's a keeper."

Shelby revved the engine of her Jeep checked her mirrors and pulled into the street, hoping she wouldn't get hung up at the county's only stoplight. She hurried as much as she dared, desperate to make it to Jones' office inside his deadline. She glanced at the clock – less than four minutes.

Half a block up the street, the light turned amber, then to red. Shelby stared at it in disbelief. For no apparent reason, the traffic-activated stoplight had changed despite the fact that there was no cross traffic in sight. Braking to a stop, Shelby gasped "Questions! I need three *intelligent* questions!" She paused, and then took advantage of the moment to quiet her mind. "Dear Lord, please help me learn the right info for this story," she said quietly. Then she opened her eyes and inhaled slowly. The light changed to green. Shelby looked left and right. She had been the only person at the intersection. There was no reason for that light to have been red. No reason at all – except that Shelby had needed to slow down and think before arriving at Mr. Jones' office.

By Shelby's clock she made it to the door of the office with about 15 seconds to spare. She rapped assertively on the door and waited for a reply. She took a deep breath and rapped a second time. "Miss Sweetin, you had better get yourself in here little lady or you will miss your last chance to interview me," boomed the gruff voice of Arthur Jones.

Shelby pushed the door open, tried to combine a hurried entrance with a touch of grace, and plastered on a queen contestant smile. "Good morning, Mr. Jones. Thank you for seeing me this morning. I hope I didn't keep you waiting … I just got your message." Shelby was babbling and she knew it. Her mind flickered to the image of Steven No-name rambling during the meeting the previous evening, and she realized that she should be kinder in her judgment of the man. He had been speaking to a crowd after all, and here she was, struggling to put together a coherent sentence while speaking privately with

Mr. Jones. Shelby paused and focused on Arthur, who was staring at her in disbelief and mild amusement.

The man was seated behind a massive dark wood desk. He wore a dark conservative suit, white dress shirt buttoned to the neck and a no-nonsense tie. He regarded her over his reading glasses as only his eyes moved. "You fluster easily, don't you?" he asked mildly. Suddenly he gestured toward the chair to Shelby's left, "You'd better sit down – that is if you plan to take notes," he growled. She wondered at the man's transformation from the refined orator he'd been during the meeting to the gruff, impatient man before her now. His manner changed again and he asked "How are you this morning, Miss Sweetin?"

Shelby reminded herself that a person would always catch more flies with honey than with vinegar, as her mother used to say. Shelby stepped forward and extended her right hand toward the brusque man. "Why, I am just fine," Shelby chimed in response, "And how …," Shelby remembered Bobbie's advice just in time to convert her question into a statement. "I am just thrilled that you invited me here today." Shelby paused again and smiled with genuine warmth.

Mr. Jones' face began to transform and a faint gurgling sound came from deep in his chest. He was shaking now, with laughter, and the effect reminded Shelby of Santa Claus and a bowl full of jelly reference. She giggled slightly, feeling more relaxed. When Mr. Jones stopped the laughter as suddenly as it had begun, he said, "You nearly wasted one of your precious questions, Missy. You ready to get down to business?"

Shelby regarded Mr. Jones as she hung her coat over the back of the chair and got her notebook out. She needed to find a way to get Mr. Jones to divulge a lot of information, but she would have to be careful in the way she went about it, since he had been very clear that he would only answer three questions. "Yes, sir. I'd like the name of the man who spoke against the project last night," she said.

Mr. Jones didn't move, but Shelby had a sense that he was squirming mentally. He finally said, "There are people who are opposed anything that's new or progressive. They want things to stay just the way they have always been."

Shelby watched Mr. Jones expectantly. She raised her eyebrows as Mr. Jones finally added. "You'd do well to disregard his comments. I don't generally like to speak badly of people, but no one respects him. He's a wild card and could derail the project if his mindless ranting take root in the community."

The pen against paper made the slightest scratching noise as Shelby began to record Mr. Jones' statement. "What do you think you are doing?" boomed the voice from across the desk. Shelby was startled to see wrath in the glint of Mr. Jones' eye when she glanced up. "That was off the record. You can't print that!" he growled as he leaped to his feet.

Shelby swallowed hard. The man was as intimidating as she imagined a raging elephant would be. Shelby flushed as she felt the age old fight or flight instinct kick in. She couldn't run, and fighting Mr. Jones looked like a losing proposition. Then the words from Proverbs echoed in her mind, *better a patient man than a warrior, a man who controls his temper than one who takes a city*. "Ah, Mr. Jones, we seem to have gotten started on a bad note," Shelby said while she remained seated. She consciously tried to be calm as she continued, "As I learned in my journalism classes at the university, when a statement is going to be off the record, the interviewee needs to clarify that prior to making the statement."

Mr. Jones had retreated to his high-backed chair; his color was returning to normal. Shelby cleared her throat and moved forward on her chair slightly. "Seeing as how you and I aren't quite used to each other as yet, I'll take your previous statement as off the record. But please, Mr. Jones, moving forward, let's try to adhere to the notion that off the record statements must be preceded by saying so prior making the statement."

Mr. Jones appeared to ponder that for a moment, and then leaning forward said, "Fair enough. Now do you or do you not have your three questions ready?"

"Yes, I'll get to them. But first, I would like you to explain the plan to pay for the proposed football stadium and track complex," she stated. Mr. Jones chortled once again, and said, "Miss Sweetin, I do believe you can call me Arthur." And that set the tone for the rest of the interview.

Forty minutes later Shelby had finally used up her three questions, sprinkled among numerous leading statements. She possessed a substantial set of notes from which to write her story. Mr. Jones - Arthur - had also provided schematic drawings, architects' reports and budget reports to augment her story. He had concluded the interview by reminding Shelby of the importance of positive press for promoting projects that improve the community. As she left Jones' office, Shelby thought with humor that the man was about as subtle as a heart attack, but she was forced to acknowledge that he was worthy of respect.

Shelby was speeding back toward the office when the stoplight ahead changed to amber, and then to red. Shelby shook her head in dismay as she braked to stop. Not quite déjà vu. This time there was a bright blue Chevy pickup pulling into the intersection. The driver was sandy haired and amber eyed. He turned to look Shelby in the eye as he passed in front of her vehicle. Time slowed and Shelby's mind registered that the driver looked happy as all get out as he grinned widely and winked at her. Riley!

And then he was through the intersection and gone. A horn blared behind her. Amazed to find that she was causing a traffic jam in a one-horse town, Shelby accelerated and proceeded down the street. Two right turns and she was back at the office. She smiled as she recalled the morning's events. She had earned the respect of Bobbie and Arthur; obtained excellent material for her story, and she had seen Riley again. Things were definitely looking up!

Cadee Brystal

CHAPTER FOUR

Riley was well aware that he'd told the new reporter from the Chronicle that he was sorry for embarrassing her Monday night. Now, barely twelve hours later, he had just gone and winked at her again, and he enjoyed it! As his truck rolled down the street, he recalled her look of surprise as he passed through the intersection. Was it his imagination, or did she start to blush again from his drive-by-wink?

Riley and his buddies, Matt and Tyler, had stopped in at the community meeting about the school's proposed athletic complex in a specific attempt to be good citizens. To be involved, be informed, be leaders in the future of their hometown. Well, people had been giving them the "what the world are you doing here?" look during the entire meeting. But that hadn't been the worst part. The worst part was when he heard the word "troublemakers" and he turned to see who had said it and about whom. He found it was Mrs. Fields, who was talking to the slight little blonde with the notepad and the dismayed expression.

Riley had been pigeon-holed as a troublemaker since early grade school. It wasn't fair, and it wasn't right. Sure, he and his friends indulged in numerous mischievous activities as they passed through their youth – but nothing serious. Still, growing up in a small town on the plains of South Dakota, Riley often felt like he was living under a microscope. Sometimes a young man just has to do something to startle the people looking down through the lenses.

Since Riley, Matt and Tyler finished their studies in the regional vocational technical institute, they had returned to Miller's Bend and set about being responsible adults. The problem was sometimes the townspeople who watched you grow up, won't let you *be* grown up. And so, when Riley heard the word "troublemakers", he zeroed in on the conversation. In a heartbeat he reacted in his old style by stirring things up just a little.

If I'm going to be called a troublemaker, I may as well do something, right? Riley flashed on the thought so quickly and responded out of habit. Too fast to give it a second thought, he produced a wicked grin and winked at the serious woman who worked as a Boy Friday – like the servant in *Robinson Crusoe* – for the local weekly newspaper. And she responded with such an astonished look that he immediately felt shame for his actions.

Oh, but what an impressive blush the woman possessed. It began with a deepening of the light pink skin tone, and then bloomed into a full, rich rosiness. He could have sworn that her pretty little face was still getting redder as she let her hair down to shield her face. He felt truly chagrined to have provoked such a response in the poor girl. He hadn't meant to embarrass her – he just … What had he intended? *Oh, yeah. To give Mrs. Fields reason to believe that he was still a troublemaker after all. Brilliant, Riley. Way to prove you've matured!*

Riley pulled into a parking space at the struggling manufacturing business where he was employed, and set his mind on his work. Carrying the supplies he had been sent to get, Riley was met by the owner, Daryl. "Get everything?" he asked dubiously.

"Of course," Riley responded.

"Hmm, let me see," Daryl countered while beginning to search through the box. "Looks right. How'd you get all that done so fast?" he growled. Daryl was old. Probably well past the age when he could have retired if he'd worked at the local plant for decades. Daryl had instead taken the entrepreneurial route through life - setting his own pace and letting his clients set his pay scale. As a result, he hadn't bankrolled the funds needed to retire.

"Fast?"

"Yeah, fast. If I'd have sent Steven it would have taken until noon before I'd have seen the whites of his eyes again," Daryl explained. He wiped some grease from his work-hardened hands, returned the shop rag to his pocket and reached for the box of supplies. As he turned to away, he muttered something that sounded a lot like "nice and reliable".

Riley grinned. He sure did like the way it made him feel when he could surprise his gruff old boss and get a complement. "Well, I guess your expectations are lower than they should be," Riley shot as he headed toward the welding area to work on the hay feeders that needed to be finished and shipped by Thursday. As he rounded the corner Daryl was looking after him with a strange expression. A very strange expression, indeed.

The morning passed quickly and when the small crew took a break in early afternoon, Riley approached Daryl in the office. "I've been thinking," he began cautiously. Daryl glanced up at the young man and seemed to be assessing him.

"Come in. Shut the door," the old man replied. Riley glanced back toward the other workers gathered around a flimsy table in the corner of the showroom. Doubts rose up in his mind - maybe he should just keep his thoughts to himself and go hang with the guys. How Daryl chose to run his business wasn't really any of Riley's concern. As the younger man hesitated, Daryl cleared his throat, "Something's on your mind. Spit it out."

Riley gently closed the door, then moved forward and slid into the chair in the corner of the cramped box that served as Daryl's office. It was dirty and grungy, but being located in a metal fabrication plant, that was to be expected – wasn't it? Or was it? Maybe that was another thing that could be changed to help the business. Clean up out front, haul away the broken down "stuff" piled out back, and apply a new coat of paint on the building, put up some signage, display their product better … Riley's list of ideas went on.

"Riley. Your break's gonna be over and all you'll have done is warm up that chair," Daryl observed with a slight crook to his mouth. Then he grew serious, "You've got to spit it out, boy, I don't read minds. Well, sometimes Millie thinks I do, but she's wrong – dead wrong." Daryl's gaze wandered to the framed photo of his wife and kids, long since grown and gone their own ways in the world.

Now it was Riley's turn to bring Daryl back to the present situation. "I've been thinking…"

"So you said," Daryl retorted.

"You know I took the welding and design classes in tech school," Riley began again. Daryl nodded, as he began to feel a sense of dread. Riley was a good employee, and this sounded like the beginning of an "I'm going on to bigger and better things" speech. "I don't know if you're aware of it, but I also took some business management classes …"

"Now wait a minute," the older man cut Riley off. "I don't want to lose you. You're a good worker – conscientious, hard-working, reliable and honest." He got up and paced to the door, placing his hand against it as though attempting to assure that the others didn't hear. "I can pay you a bit more, if it'll keep you here," he said quietly.

Riley was shocked and it took a moment for him to realize that his boss had taken his words to mean he was thinking about leaving. "That would be nice," he said with a smile. "But I won't hold you to it. That's not where I was headed."

"Where are you headed, Riley?" the old man said on a sigh. "I don't just mean with this conversation, either. Have you finally found God's direction for your future?"

"I … I …," Riley stammered. His brow furrowed as the question made him wonder if that was what he'd been feeling recently. Was God trying to steer his direction? He had been feeling a lot of things lately. Things like embarrassment over some of his behavior. Activities that used to be mainstays in his life didn't hold the same appeal. And lately he'd been going to church on Sunday even though his mother had long since quit nagging him about it. He even volunteered to help with the Sunday school kids. He thought the changes were just a sign of growing up, but … "I'm not sure I understand," he finally confessed.

The men both remained silent for a moment. "Well, there are men who go through life looking for a good time," Daryl began to explain. "Then there are men who go through good times while looking for a life." His eyes had strayed to the photo of his family again. "Sometimes it takes a long time to find your real life. Too long," he said.

"I know you've had your fun. Your share and somebody else's, too, if I don't miss my guess," Daryl observed. Riley thought the room was getting awfully small, and hot. He grew uneasy under Daryl's scrutiny. This was going all wrong. This is not the conversation Riley wanted to be having. He jumped to his feet, needing to get out of the office – to get away.

"My break's over. Gotta go," he blurted as he bolted for the office door.

"Wait a minute," Daryl said. "Your break goes another five minutes at least, maybe more if you want to talk about a business plan," he said glancing at the clock on the wall. It was one of those old fashioned ones – vintage – a tuxedo cat with the eyes that flicked back and forth, keeping time like the hands of a metronome. "This time you assumed that I was heading somewhere other than where I was a'going."

Riley froze and waited. "Like I said you're a good employee," Daryl offered, backtracking in the conversation. He was certain that the changes he'd seen in Riley were the reflection of God's influence in the young man's soul, but it was clear that Riley wasn't ready to talk about it. At least not with him. "What I mean to tell you is that I am proud to have you as part of this business. I've seen changes in you since you went off to school. You've matured, but there's more to it," Daryl paused, gauging Riley's reaction.

Riley, who had stopped in mid-stride, had relaxed a bit and turned to face Daryl once more. Daryl read in his expression an interesting mix of confusion, curiosity, pride, and a longing. "I think we better talk business now, if you are still of a mind to," the boss suggested. "I'd really like to hear your ideas." Riley assessed the older man once more. Then his gaze caught on the family photo again. He got a strong feeling that Daryl had been through some things in life that could help Riley in his own quests if he was willing to listen and learn.

"Yes, sir," Riley cleared his throat. "I have some ideas that might help the business."

Cadee Brystal

CHAPTER FIVE

Shelby stood just inside the door of the Daily Dose. She smiled broadly at Karla, the owner, and sent a wave her way. As her focus traveled around the seating area, Shelby's glance stopped briefly at Riley's table and then swung back around the room again. She scowled for a second and then started toward Riley.

He had discreetly watched her sweep the room for the client she was sent to meet. She wore a very purposeful, professional expression when she'd entered. It turned friendly while she greeted Karla, and then it had morphed into confusion as she saw all the empty seats. Finally, there was dismay as she registered that Riley was the only person there.

Riley stood to greet the intriguing young woman as she moved gracefully toward him. He extended his hand and a charming smile graced his face, "Hi, I'm Riley Wheeler." Shelby paused, shifted her bag on her shoulder and placed her delicate hand into his. Neither spoke immediately as some instinct drove Riley to tighten his hold on her. A whisper of a thought passed through him so quickly that he wasn't sure he hadn't imagined it. *Never let her go.*

Shelby's mind had stalled out when Riley had enveloped her hand in his larger, much warmer one. Belatedly she realized that he had introduced himself and was looking at her expectantly. "Shelby Sweetin," she responded. "May I sit with you until my client arrives?" Riley pulled a chair out and indicated she should sit. Then he returned to his own chair.

"You can stay right here and have lunch with me," he said with his eyes twinkling. As though he suddenly realized that he had leaned forward across the table while making the offer, he retreated. Pushing back in his chair and carelessly tossing his arm across the adjacent one, he sighed, "Unless you have something better to do?"

"No, I'm sorry, I have a business lunch scheduled," she countered. "Perhaps another time ..." Her voice faded out as she noted the notebook on the table in front of Riley and the confidence emanating from the man. It was as though he knew she didn't have "something better to do". But she did. She had a business lunch planned to discuss the Southside Industries account. Suspicion flared in her expression as she began to realize something was off. *Oh, no. No, no, no. Riley cannot be the client!*

Riley beamed as he saw the awareness dawn on Shelby. She was beginning to understand that he was the client she had been sent to meet for lunch. Shelby's spine stiffened. She'd been ambushed and she didn't like it – not at all. And then a soft laugh escaped from the handsome man before her. His laughter was deep and warm and far too intimate. And it made her feel suddenly very warm and ... out of control. For the second time that day she felt the fight or flight urge and this time she chose flight. She pushed her chair back and stood as she reached for her coat.

"I'm afraid there's been a mistake," she said fiercely. The fire was back in those crystal blue eyes. The image reminded him of fire on the water – a contradiction as amazing as Shelby herself. And, although he really wanted to tease her, push her just a little more, Riley reached out, touching her hand. "Please sit down," he offered calmly. "Let's order and I'll explain."

Karla was suddenly beside the table to take their orders. Riley ordered a chocolate shake and the special - a sandwich called Reuben Done Wrong. Then he and Karla looked expectantly toward Shelby. She sighed inwardly. If Riley was the client, she needed to hear him out. If he wasn't, then she needed to stay and see if the real client showed up. In either case she needed to eat. Pulling up a smile for Karla, she ordered a fruit bowl and water. Slowly she settled back into her chair. The pair watched as Karla retreated to the food prep area before they turned back to each other.

"My boss –" both began to speak and then suddenly stopped. The smile that broke across Riley's face was endearing, causing Shelby to look away. When she glanced back up at Riley, he graciously said, "Go ahead, please."

"My boss sent me to meet with a client about a new promotion plan for his business," she explained. "I'm to have lunch with Daryl from the manufacturing company south of town." Her brow furrowed, "I expected a much older man, whose name is most definitely not Riley." It was vital to Shelby that her boss regard her as a competent professional who could be counted on not only to bring in the news, but also new clients for advertising revenue. "I'd better call the office and see how I've messed this up," she said absently as she started rifling through her bag in search of her cell phone. "I've got to fix this."

Once again Riley reached for her hand to stop Shelby, thinking that she was definitely a flighty one. "Daryl sent me in his place," he said in explanation. "I work with ... for Daryl at Southside Industries."

Shelby stared, disbelief clearly written on her features. "Did you set this up just to try to meet me?" she queried. "Did Catherine know you would be here instead of Daryl?"

"I'm here on business," Riley ground out in response to the words that hit him like an insult. "If I wanted to date you I would call you up and ask you out."

"I didn't say you wanted to date me!" Shelby countered with growing apprehension. "I just don't understand why you are here. All of a sudden you are everywhere – the meeting last night, the intersection and now you are miraculously my lunch partner. Do you expect me to believe it's all a coincidence?"

"I don't care what you believe," Riley bit out in reply. He stiffened in the chair and looked out the window while trying to remain calm. Shelby glanced around the tiny coffee shop. Everything in this place was perfectly typical of small towns and rural life, at least as far as she would know. She had never lived in a community bigger than Brookings, where she had attended the university four years.

Suspicion burned through Shelby's mind. She had seen friends in college who had trusted men too quickly and too completely. Some had suffered life-long consequences from their foolish innocence. She had watched and learned, and once she'd gotten the lesson, she wasn't likely to forget it.

Riley's eyes were back on her again. Shelby studied the man before her, trying to judge him. Was he trustworthy? But he'd closed off the friendly look that had been there before. He seemed to be studying a spot in the distance, behind Shelby's right ear. He looked annoyed. No, more than annoyed – hurt, maybe. Then in flash that emotion was gone and he looked back to Shelby's face.

"I don't need you to insult me. I came to talk business. If the paper doesn't need Daryl's business, I'm sure that Vanessa from the Shopper would be happy to have it," he suggested with an eerie calm.

Shelby's mind flashed back to the time she and Bobbie had been walking toward their cars after work and saw Vanessa clinging to a businessman as they left the bar. Well, clinging to each other was a more accurate description. Bobbie had spoken quietly, "She gets the ad sales alright, but at what price?" and then added a "tsk, tsk, tsk" as she shook her head disapprovingly. "He'll have a full page ad in the Shopper in the next week or two," she had accurately predicted.

Shelby felt suddenly sick. She looked down at her hands and back up to Riley. A sense of shock rocked Shelby as she pictured Vanessa wrapping herself around Riley. *Oh, no you don't.* She struggled to convince herself that she didn't care in the slightest what Riley did in his personal life. Her only concern should be to get the business for the newspaper. It was purely professional concern. And then a long-forgotten Bible verse came to mind: Let not your heart envy sinners, but continue in the fear of the Lord all the day.

"That won't be necessary," she said defiantly. She very deliberately pulled her blue and green paisley print three ring binder from her bag. She set it before her on the table and retrieved a gold pen from her plum colored bag with a huge flower imprinted in dark purple. The design was livened up with white spirals. She clicked the pen on, off, then on again. Then with the rodeo queen smile she had perfected, she looked Riley in the eye and said, "Tell me what you and Daryl have in mind."

Their food arrived and something in the atmosphere changed. They were like any other people having a business lunch. Discussion about ideas to promote Southside Industries bounced between the pair. Other diners had come and gone. The little coffee shop once again held only Riley and Shelby. When Karla appeared with the check, Shelby was startled, having forgotten that they weren't alone. Riley quickly handed over a credit card and flashed Karla a radiant smile as he announced, "I've got it."

Karla snatched the card and disappeared before Shelby gathered her wits to respond, "I pay my own way."

Riley regarded her quietly. "Next time," he said as he stood and moved behind Shelby's chair to help her into her coat.

"Ah ... I don't ..." She sputtered to a halt. Of course there would be a next time – if she got the account. "That will do nicely. Thank you," she answered demurely.

Tuesday proceeded in a crazy, chaotic rush. Shelby hurried back to the newspaper office with her head full of Riley Wheeler and his ideas for improving another man's business. She pushed those thoughts aside and returned her focus to the big story about the school board's public meeting Monday night. She had composed the first draft before lunch and reviewed it now.

As she scanned the type, she came to the spot where she quoted Steven No-name. "Crud," she breathed on a sigh. How was she going to get his name? She cradled her head in her hands.

"Shelby! Phone's for you – line two!" Catherine's time-roughened shout rang above the office buzz.

She seized the receiver and jerked it to her ear, "Hi, this is Shelby," she chimed, only to be met by silence. "Hello?"

"Hi, Shelby. It's Riley," the caller identified himself. "I forgot to mention that we need to advertise across the border … you know into Minnesota. Can you figure something for that, too?"

"Sure thing, I'll get you some numbers," she responded cheerfully. Then she heard yelling in the background of the call. It sounded like swearing. She frowned thinking there is never a reason for swearing – especially in the workplace.

"Hold on Steven, I'll be right there," Riley's voice announced, but it was muffled as though his hand covered the mouthpiece. "Shelby? I gotta go, I'll call you later," he directed toward her.

"Wait!" she yelled.

"Yes?" he answered. Was that cockiness she heard in his voice?

"You were at the community meeting Monday," Shelby said, almost a question, but still a declarative.

"You know I was," Riley answered thinking again of the blush she had produced after the wink he'd sent her way.

"Do you know Steven's last name? The big, sweaty guy ..." she clapped her hand to her forehead and rolled her eyes. "I mean the gentleman who addressed the group with some opposition to the project?" she asked. She bit her lip as she waited for Riley to respond.

"Yeah, I know his name," Riley said shortly. "Why?"

"For the story, I didn't get his name that night," she explained. *Because I was distracted by you!*

"Miller."

"Miller? Steven Miller? Like the old Steve Miller Band?" Shelby exclaimed. "You have got to be kidding!"

"Bend, not band," Riley responded. "Miller's Bend is named for Steven's family. They settled the town."

They wrapped up the conversation and Shelby considered how to handle the new information. So the only person to speak against the school's proposed new athletic complex was Steven. Steven Miller - a descendent of the town's founders. But, was he a person who was respected or despised? Would his words matter to the readers or would they think Shelby was foolish to include the things Steven had said? Shelby didn't know what to do. Great. Just great.

Shelby remembered Arthur Jones' words, "You really need to learn who's who and what's what or you may as well go running home ..." Was Steven one of the people to whom Arthur was referring? Shelby worried because in a small town, sometimes certain topics or certain people were untouchable. What were the implications of quoting Steven in the story? Would the paper be in trouble? Would she be in trouble?

And what would happen if she didn't quote Steven? He was the only person to take the stage speaking against the proposed athletic complex. Everyone present in the audience, as well as all of the board members, would know that she had left out an important part of the story. It would be easy to promote the complex. That was what Mr. Jones was after – "positive press about projects that improve the community."

Shelby stared at the computer monitor. Steven No-Name's statements were accurate and raised some legitimate questions about the project. He had not spoken eloquently, but he had spoken from the point of view many school district residents might have taken - if they had shown the fortitude to stand up on in front of the gathering and express themselves.

But as soon as Shelby deleted the "e-m-a-N---o-N" one keystroke at a time, and typed M-i-l-l-e-r in its place, she began to panic. Does it really matter who he is? Is he well respected? Will Steven's words have greater impact because of his ancestry than if the words belonged to some other speaker? Will it wreck the board's plans for the complex? Should the project go through without these questions being asked?

Shelby closed her eyes. She pictured the instructor from her newswriting classes at the university. "You will be the story tellers," he had said. "You must tell the whole story, not just the easy parts of the story." Shelby knew in her heart that reporters are called upon to report everything, not just the nice, clean little package that the people of position try to sell to the public.

Arthur would be angry if Steven's words caused others to question his plan. Shelby worried that she could lose Mr. Jones as a news source if he became upset with her. She put her head into the bowl of her hands again. Her shoulders were tense, her neck ached and now Shelby's head was beginning to pound. It was a definite tension headache.

As Shelby sat at her desk, watching the cursor blink, she thought about the implications of taking the easy route, versus taking the right route. She remembered visiting with Mrs. Holmes and how the kindly old lady had been concerned that Shelby not let herself become a tool of the powerful. And a verse from Proverbs popped into her mind: Truthful words stand the test of time, but lies are soon exposed. News stories need to stand the test of time. They become archived and years from now people will look back on the story. They would read her words and believe them to be the truth. Therefore, she must write the truth, not just the pretty little presentation that had been prepared by Mr. Jones and the school board.

Shelby stood and stretched out her arms and rotated her neck to ease the tension. She had a lot more work to do before press time.

CHAPTER SIX

The following morning Catherine was speaking with someone on the telephone when Shelby arrived in the 100-year-old newspaper office. It was even older than that – Shelby had learned that the building was constructed as a bank prior to 1880. Naturally, there had been renovations, but key pieces made the interior unique. There was antique woodwork with intricate scroll designs throughout the building, and decorative tin graced the ceiling. A cobbled floor was laid in the lobby and work areas many decades earlier, and had been well maintained through the years.

Catherine was a puzzle to Shelby. She was a brusque and demanding woman, always positive that her own point of view was the right one. She had made her way in the business world when the vast majority of her peers desired nothing more than to marry and raise babies. She chose to go off to college. And then, partly because her father had the means, she traveled to Washington and worked in the nation's capital, covering the news and making acquaintances that would be her network for decades to come.

She even traveled alone for several weeks when she was in her 20s, which was an extraordinarily uncommon occurrence at that time. Now, rotund, yet deeply wrinkled, the charismatic Catherine loved to retell the tales to her staff during daily coffee breaks. Shelby would listen raptly, wondering what it was like for those who feel the pull for adventure – the wanderers. As a young adult, Catherine had sojourned to the Pacific Northwest and then proceeded to tour the West Coast, traveling into Mexico. She moved along the Gulf Coast to New Orleans. From there she returned home to South Dakota.

Shelby was envious of those who had the spirit to do such things. While she was content to stay much, much closer to home, she often wished that she found such travel rewarding or even appealing.

As she went about getting to work, Shelby was able to overhear snatches of Catherine's side of the telephone conversation: "sorry that you're upset", "no, I will not", "stand behind it unconditionally", "that's just fine" and "I'll see you then."

Shelby's stomach clenched as a feeling of dread overtook her. She was absolutely certain the conversation had to do with her story about the school district's proposed athletic complex. Shelby shed her winter coat, gloves and scarf, and hung them on the rack. She booted up her computer and greeted Bobbie.

"Shelby, come up here," Catherine summoned when she had disconnected the call. Shelby obediently moved to appear at Catherine's desk. "That was Mr. Jones," she said as she indicated the telephone on her desk. "He's got a head of steam on this morning." Catherine studied Shelby a moment. "I trust everything in your story about the athletic complex is accurate?" she queried squinting slightly as she studied Shelby.

Shelby nodded, "Yes, ma'am."

"And you can prove it if you have to?" Catherine added with her brows raised.

"Yes, ma'am," Shelby repeated. Her heart was racing. She was beginning to dread what was ahead. "Do you want me to get my notes and recording from the meeting?" she asked as she began moving toward her desk for the items.

"Oh heavens, no," Catherine answered. "Jones will get his way in the end - he's just mad right now. He'll get over it. Take a ten out of the till and go get some caramel rolls, would you?"

And that was it. Shelby moved to the coat rack and wrapped the warm knitted scarf around her neck, silently thanking her sister, Sally, for making it for her. She slid her arms into the winter coat she had shed only minutes before and headed for the door.

She breathed in the crisp fresh air as she walked to the Daily Dose to retrieve the requested caramel rolls for the staff and a cola for herself. Jones was mad; Catherine would support Shelby. There would be more meetings and more news stories, but it looked as though Shelby could handle it. She stepped into the coffee shop which had about a half dozen patrons seated and a massive man at the counter picking up a to-go order.

Even with his back to her, he seemed familiar. As he turned away from the counter, toward Shelby, the smile he had given Karla faded. "You're the new gal at the paper, right?" he asked.

"That's right," she said as she stepped forward and extended her hand. "Shelby Sweetin."

The man looked at her. He paused and the background noise stopped abruptly. Then as he took her hand and shook it slowly, he said, "I'm Steven Miller, it's nice to meet you."

"Yes, I know. You spoke during the community meeting Monday night," Shelby replied. "Will you be at the next meeting?"

"I suspect so," the large man grunted in reply. "I'll be better prepared. I read your story this morning."

Shelby waited. She tried to think of an appropriate response. Thank you? What did you think? Did she really want to know what he thought? She waited, as did the people around them who had stopped chatting, stopped eating, and stopped drinking their coffee.

"I should thank you," Steven said quietly. "Some people wouldn't have cared what I had to say. Or what anyone but the board members had to say, for that matter. Thank you." Then he moved quickly toward the door.

Steven's rapid departure left Shelby standing midway between the door and the counter, with all eyes on her. She glanced from table to table, from face to face, smiling as she did so. "Good morning, everyone," she sang out as she moved to the counter. "I'll need four caramel rolls, Karla," Shelby stated as she neared the counter and passed the payment.

"Looks like life's going to get interesting around here," Karla commented as she glanced out the window before accepting the ten dollar bill. Shelby's eyes followed Karla's glance to see Riley and Steven talking outside the large plate glass window. It didn't look like a friendly discussion – not at all friendly. Then the two parted ways and Shelby accepted the change and the gooey rolls. "I drizzled some extra caramel on your rolls," Karla added as Shelby turned to go.

Marjorie Fields caught Shelby's attention from her position at a nearby table. "Miss Sweetin?" she said sweetly. "Do you have a moment?" Shelby sighed inwardly, but put a pleasant smile in place as she approached the table where Marjorie and two of her friends were seated, enjoying the comings and goings in the little coffee house.

"Yes, ma'am. What can I do for you?" Shelby responded. She was becoming much too warm wrapped up in her heavy winter coat, scarf and snow boots. There were large flakes coming down now, she saw through the window. She wondered absently just how much snow the predicted storm system would drop on the community.

"I just wanted to apologize. I misunderstood the other night when you asked me to identify Steven at the meeting," she didn't give Shelby the chance to respond. "It's just that you were staring at Riley and his crew of ne'er-do-wells, that I was absolutely certain that was who you were interested in." Then looking to her friends, rather than Shelby, she continued, "I simply couldn't believe such a nice girl would have an interest in any of *those* boys."

Shelby opened her mouth to defend Riley. Oh sure, he had riled her up – every time they spoke or even saw each other – but in her opinion he wasn't a troublemaker at all. He was trying to help Daryl improve the business; he was trying to be active in the community. But it seemed like everyone who chose to comment, always painted him as a bad boy. Of course, she'd only known him a few days and these people had known him since he learned to walk, or place frogs in little girls' lunch boxes, or whatever did on his way to growing up. Maybe he even tipped over some outhouses!

Marjorie took a sip of her coffee and pinned Shelby with a motherly look, "I do hope you don't have a taste for that type of young man. Oh, there's a nice new lawyer who moved to town. He might be good for you!" There was a twinkle in her eye and she wore a very self-satisfied expression. It was as though she had solved some looming problem that, if left unchecked, would have doomed mankind.

"Thank you Mrs. Fields, but I'm not looking for any young man," Shelby replied as she went into a full blush again. She knew it was coming and was helpless to stop it – just as helpless as she was to stop Mrs. Fields' interjection into her private life.

"Oh, poppycock! Every young lady is looking for a young man," she said, looking to her companions for confirmation. They nodded and murmured their assent.

CHAPTER SEVEN

Mercifully, the remainder of Wednesday was calm. Shelby picked up a few groceries on her way home from work and then slipped into her apartment, eager to spend a quiet evening alone. She shucked out of her work clothes and pulled on the fuzzy polka-dot pajama bottoms and fluffy sweatshirt she loved to snuggle in. She brewed her favorite flavor of tea, set her iPod to a serene playlist and grabbed the best-selling novel she had started reading over the weekend. Ahhh.

As she headed to the couch, balancing the book and the mug of tea, her phone rang, stopping Shelby in mid-stride. Glaring at the phone, she rushed to the end table where she set her supplies with a huff. The phone rang again. The tea spilled.

Shelby snatched up the phone and punched the talk button. "Hello?"

"Hello, Shelby," she was greeted by Mrs. Holmes' warm voice. "I was wondering what time you'll be ready to go."

She was at a loss as to any reason Mrs. Holmes could possibly think she would be going anywhere this evening. But before Shelby could form an inquiry, Mrs. Holmes prompted gently, "Also, I was wondering if you want to drive my car, or if you would prefer we take yours to church tonight?"

The mention of church reminded Shelby of the terms of renting the apartment from the kindly old woman. "Of course, Mrs. Holmes. My Jeep is already warm, let's take it," Shelby replied as she looked longingly at the book, the rapidly cooling tea, and the afghan that lay on the couch waiting for her. "What time do we need to leave?"

"We should have plenty of time if we leave in about a half hour," the elder lady stated.

"I'll knock on your door when I'm ready," Shelby replied.

Knowing she had no time for a shower, Shelby spritzed a little body spray to freshen up, and quickly changed clothes. As she brushed her hair and pulled it into a low pony tail, she changed her mind and formed a quick braid. Thankful that there would be no one she needed to impress at the casual church gathering, she decided that her quick preparation would be adequate.

Twenty-two minutes after the phone call from Mrs. Holmes, Shelby stood outside the main entrance of the home, knocking and shivering. The snow had continued throughout the day and with nightfall the wind picked up. The snow swirled around Shelby, a bit of it peppering her neck which was exposed. She considered returning to her apartment to retrieve her forgotten scarf, but instead she knocked again – more insistently this time – as cold began to seep through her clothing. She tried the door and it opened with a tired creak. "Mrs. Holmes?" she called loudly. "Mrs. Holmes!" Shelby repeated more forcefully.

Moving into the sitting room, Shelby spotted the elderly woman, who appeared almost as a shadow in the darkened room. "Mrs. Holmes, I'm ready to go," Shelby said, clearing her throat and stomping her feet to create extra noise, so as not to startle the woman. Her heart rate accelerated as Shelby raced to the still form in the recliner. *Oh, dear God, please let her be alright!*

Shelby quickly felt for pulse on Mrs. Holmes' throat. Her skin was papery and nearly translucent, and loose to the touch. A light but steady pulse beat beneath Shelby's fingers. She moved to take Mrs. Holmes by the hand and patted it, "Mrs. Holmes … please wake up. MaryAnn! Please!"

"Do stop yelling, dear, I was simply resting up for church you know," the tenderly spoken murmur reached Shelby, just as she was moving to get her phone from her jeans pocket. "I'm quite all right."

Shelby stared in disbelief as Mrs. Holmes transformed from the whisper of a woman to her normally frail and waif-like form. She stretched gently and seemed to test her legs before moving to lift herself from the comfort of the recliner. "Well, dear, don't just stand there," she said with a smile in her voice, "bring my coat and wind chaser, won't you?"

"How … what …," Shelby faltered. "But, I thought … Oh, Mrs. Holmes – You scared me half to death!" she finally squealed. Then realizing the travesty of using lines like that around the severely aged, she clapped her hands over her mouth. Moving to Mrs. Holmes side she began to babble, "Oh, no! Forgive me, please! I didn't mean anything by…"

Mrs. Holmes' expression was kind. Her countenance radiated peace when she responded, "Not to worry, dear. I've always slept like I was in a coma. It has nothing to do with either my age, or my mortality. Now, if it's alright with you I would prefer not to be the last to arrive at church."

Shelby carefully navigated the snow-laden streets of Miller's Bend. The cold and windy weather of the last few days had finally given way to the snowfall earlier in the day. Shelby was more than happy that Mrs. Holmes was willing to let her drive the four wheel drive Jeep instead of insisting on using her own sedan. She reflected that they surely wouldn't have made the short trip to the church if they'd opted for the car. With muscles tense, Shelby began to think they should have stayed home instead of venturing out.

"Just pull up by the door, someone will escort me inside while you go park the Jeep," Mrs. Holmes said matter-of-factly as they pulled into the parking lot of the United Methodist Church. Shelby looked at the woman, a bit concerned, because she had just been wondering how to proceed. "It happens all the time, dear. When you are a child of God, your needs are met without having to make a fuss," she offered in explanation. "You'll see."

Mrs. Holmes was out of the vehicle and standing on the curb in an amazingly quick move. She waved Shelby to go park the idling vehicle. Shelby looked around – there was no one there to take the old lady's arm and walk with her. However, Mrs. Holmes gestures grew more and more animated, so Shelby put the Jeep in gear and cruised toward the far end of the parking area to find a spot.

Shelby raced to the entrance of the church, hoping that Mrs. Holmes had been correct. The heavy, wet snow caked Shelby's boots making it difficult to move fast. She lost traction, slipping precariously a couple of times before stepping up onto the sidewalk near the massive antique double doors that looked like they had been designed to keep an army out, rather than invite the sinners and worshipers in. She scanned the area and finding no one, she hefted the door open.

There in the vestibule, stood Mrs. Holmes radiating joy as three men stood in a crescent around her. One had taken her coat and wind chaser to hang for her, one was reaching for her elbow, and one was listening to her with rapt attention. Mrs. Holmes directed her comment to Shelby, "You see, I told you God would provide exactly what I need. Riley and his friends helped me inside, just like I said!" She accentuated the comment with a radiant smile.

As the words flowed from Mrs. Holmes, the three had turned toward Shelby. Riley's face etched in anger. "What were you thinking?" Riley said lowly, but with a definite edge. Shelby's shock froze her in place as he advanced on her. "I didn't take you for a person who would dump an old lady off in a snowstorm and just drive away!" Shelby's eyes flew to Mrs. Holmes. Had she been wrong to follow the woman's wishes?

"I didn't think it was a problem. She was confident ..." Shelby began weakly.

"Obviously, you didn't think!" Riley blared. His face became an odd shade of red and he clenched his jaw as Mrs. Holmes placed her hand on his shoulder. He closed his eyes while he visibly tried to calm himself.

Riley opened his eyes, which somehow had changed from the endearing caramel brown Shelby expected to a nearly black shade, and glared at Shelby. She responded by straightening her spine, lifting her chin and returning the glare. Shelby breathed deeply in an attempt to calm herself, but moved forward, as if she was heading into battle.

"Now, now, dears," Mrs. Holmes sang in a serene tone. "Let's just back this up a step shall we?"

When neither answered, Mrs. Holmes gently shoved Riley to stand nearer to Shelby. "There are plenty of lessons in this little episode and since you are both quite intelligent, you will likely figure them out eventually upon a little time for reflection. But here's the one lesson I don't want either of you to miss, so I will spell it out."

"She left you standing in the cold and the wind – on an icy sidewalk no less. There's no excuse for that," Riley ranted as he threw his arms out, and then slammed his fists back against his own thighs. Shelby wondered as she watched in awe, questioning why the man would be so upset.

"Hush, now. You'll need to apologize for your behavior. But first you need to listen to me," Mrs. Holmes said. Shelby was intensely uncomfortable. She longed for her couch, her book, her tea, some distance from Riley. Her body began to subconsciously edge toward the door. Halting her retreat, Shelby wondered where she would go if she left, after all she had promised to attend church with Mrs. Holmes. She couldn't just abandon the old woman – Riley would probably hunt her down and glare at her some more. "Both of you need to listen, it's the same lesson and you both need it."

Mrs. Holmes stood taller than Shelby had ever thought her to be. Shelby stilled and Riley seemed to relax a bit. "My boy, I asked, no I insisted, that Shelby drop me off by the door and go park the Jeep." Riley's mouth opened on an inhalation of a breath so he could interject, but Mrs. Holmes shut him down. "You just keep it to yourself, Riley James. I'm the one talking now." Riley closed his mouth and nodded. The younger two people glanced at each other and began to smile. The old girl had something to say and there was no point in trying to stop her.

"I had Shelby drop me off so she would see that when we are in need of something, or someone, and if we trust in the Lord, he will provide for us. Sometimes he just drops the something we need or someone we need right in our path, and no matter how hard we try to ignore it," she glanced meaningfully from one to the other, "there's just no getting around it. Or them."

"I pray you two learn to see what God sets before you. These are his blessings to you," Mrs. Holmes sighed. "I needed help to get inside and he sent me Riley and my boys, just like that," she explained with a muted snap of her fingers.

"Think about what you need. Then look around and recognize what God has put in your path. See who he has added to your lives," she concluded. "Now, let's all go see if there's a pew left for us."

She turned toward Tyler and Matt who had been statue still during the exchange. "Let's go, boys," she said, swinging her arm in a wide circle. "I don't want us to be stuck in the pew ahead of Marjorie and her sidekicks."

Tyler, Matt, Shelby, Mrs. Holmes and Riley proceeded up the aisle to an open pew and began sliding deftly into their places. As Shelby scooted closer to Matt, thinking she would make more room to her right for Mrs. Holmes and Riley, she realized that Riley had disappeared from their procession. She glanced around to try to see what had become of the fifth member of their party. "It's okay, Shelby, he's sitting with his family," Mrs. Holmes whispered quietly. "It's very important to him to be with them during services, but he'll rejoin us again." Shelby's face flamed as she realized that she had been far too obvious in her curiosity over Riley Wheeler.

Riley settled into the pew with his parents and brother, Andrew. His family was small and they felt lucky to be close. Andrew was two years older than Riley, and at 27, continued to be the no-nonsense son. He earned exceptional grades and accolades all through his school years. Graduating in the top five percent of his class, he had gone on to college to study business and finance. Since returning to Miller's Bend, Andrew was building a reputation as an investment and financial advisor. The man was well-liked and respected in the community, and Riley was happy for Andrew, although at times he also felt a bit jealous.

Now as the foursome sat solemnly in the pew across the aisle and slightly behind the pew where Shelby had settled with Mrs. Holmes, Riley stared in their direction. Shelby's beautiful complexion had turned a burning crimson again, spiking his interest and curiosity. Riley didn't like seeing Shelby settle next to Matt, but it had really tortured him when she scooted even closer. The idea that she might like one of his best friends nettled as Riley stared. He cataloged what he saw: Tyler had taken his seat; Matt had left space beside Tyler and then sat himself. Shelby had claimed a spot, but then slid close to Matt. They were touching from her shoulder, down her arm – probably from thigh to knee, too. Then Mrs. Holmes had left a space and landed on the pew like an autumn leaf fluttering to the earth.

An elbow to the ribs from Andrew brought Riley's attention back to his family. "What?" Riley growled. He pulled his gaze away from the scene across the aisle and swiveled toward Andrew.

"You're drooling," Andrew observed quietly then looked pointedly to where Riley's attention had been snared. "And I hope it's not over Mrs. Holmes," he said as his grin expanded to an annoying degree. Then the pastor's voice filled the sanctuary and the Wednesday evening service began.

Riley caught Shelby and Mrs. Holmes near the exit after the service and the supper. "I'm sorry for my behavior earlier," he said to Mrs. Holmes as he helped her into her vintage winter coat.

Mrs. Holmes sighed, "So close, and yet so far," she said quietly. She turned to look fully at Riley, placing her hand on his forearm. "Try again," she said gesturing toward Shelby. When Riley didn't respond, the line of the old lady's eyebrows rose to accentuate the message in her eyes. People filed by, saying their good-nights as they headed home. Bewildered, Riley looked at Mrs. Holmes, and then slowly, his gaze shifted to the nervous Shelby.

She had the car keys in her gloved hand and was in an obvious rush to get going. Her need to escape was visible, now that he looked, she nearly vibrated with energy. "I'm going to go get the Jeep, I will pick you up at the curb," she said as she turned toward the exit. She paused and looked back at Riley, "Will you stay with her, please?"

Ouch! Riley jumped, pulling away from Mrs. Holmes' grasp. The frail, sweet little old lady that everybody loved had just pinched his wrist with a vicious twist! Clearly she was trying to convey some oblique message to him, but Riley wasn't getting it. "Riley, I believe your footwear is warmer than Shelby's, perhaps you would bring the car up while we ladies wait here? Where it's warm," the elder suggested weakly. She proceeded to look at Riley for a long moment, and then batted her pale gray eyelashes, playing the damsel in distress.

Andrew appeared, sweeping up to Mrs. Holmes, "I'd be happy to drive you home, if you need a lift," he suggested. He thumped his brother a little too soundly on the shoulder and offered, "I'm not sure Riley is thinking clearly just now." Andrew looked meaningfully toward Shelby and extended his hand toward her, "I'm Andrew Wheeler, Riley's brother."

As Shelby took his brother's hand and introduced herself, jealousy snaked through Riley. First Matt, now Andrew. What was it about Shelby that raised these feelings?

Riley realized with a jerk that Mrs. Holmes had been trying to get him to offer to go out in the storm and get the Jeep, so Shelby could stay inside. But there was something else, the woman wanted him to grasp and he hadn't been able to decipher it yet. "No Andrew, you make sure Mom and Dad make it home alright," Riley said, clearing his throat and straightening his stance. "I will take care of Shelby and Mrs. Holmes." Then noting the rising color in Shelby's cheeks, he addressed her, "That is, if you will allow me to." She nodded briefly as she handed the keys to him.

After Riley trekked through the snow, started the engine to warm the Jeep, cleared the windshield and arrived at the curb by the church doors, he helped the two ladies into the vehicle. "The streets are bound to be bad, judging by the parking lot," he observed. "I'll follow you back to the house to be sure you get there alright."

Shelby, positioned in the driver's seat, looked up through the open window and nodded. She was proud and self-sufficient, but not foolish. At least she hoped she wasn't foolish. It made sense to have an escort in this sort of weather. "Thank you," she answered. With her foot firmly on the brake, she shifted the vehicle into drive, and looked forward out the windshield. The snow was building up on the glass again. "We better head out."

"Shelby," Riley paused. She looked up into his eyes. Time froze. Her cheeks were brilliant pink from the cold, loose hair tendrils whipped around her face, her mouth suspended as though she had been about to speak, a question formed in her eyes and snowflakes graced her eyelashes. "I ... I am sorry that I yelled at you earlier," he said quietly. "I had no right. I have no rights at all where you are concerned." And he was gone.

Cadee Brystal

CHAPTER EIGHT

Days later, Riley made a quick stop at the auto parts store to pick up supplies for Southside Industries. He shook his head in disbelief as he and Rob looked in unison to the doorway where the bell indicating a customer's arrival sounded. It seemed to Riley that the new newspaper girl was everywhere.

Since Wednesday evening, he had noticed her numerous times either driving the fire engine red Jeep, or in nearly every business he had been in. With amusement, he considered that she could be a crazy person who was stalking him. Then with a smile he considered that he, himself may be going crazy. A frown darkened his expression as he considered those options. Mrs. Holmes' words echoed in his mind, *recognize who God has brought into your lives.* His expression deepened to a full-blown scowl. Riley didn't want anyone else in his life - yet.

Shelby exuded friendliness and openness in every situation Riley had seen her in – except in her dealings with him. She either wanted to argue with him or behave like he had some communicable disease and stay away from him all together. Of course he had set the tone for their relationship by publicly embarrassing her before he even knew her name. Then he had scolded her for leaving Mrs. Holmes in the snow at the church door. Shelby had been certain that she had been tricked when they met for lunch to discuss the promotion of Southside Industries. She'd been right, but he wasn't going to tell her that little tidbit – not now, not ever.

Riley silently tracked her progress from the entrance to the sales counter. Today she wore dark blue denim jeans and a bulky sweater that looked soft as clouds. The carefully crafted garment was the crystal blue of a summer sky on the prairie and the combination with her eye color was breathtaking. A darker blue layer, accentuated with rhinestones or something, peaked through above its neckline and drew Riley's attention to the line where fabric met skin as she drew nearer. Heat surged into his cheeks as Riley realized that he'd been staring and turned quickly toward merchandise on a table near the counter.

"Hi, Rob," she called as she approached the salesman who also served as the store manager. "How's it going today?" Her eyes drifted to Riley's and she spared him a nod and an "afternoon" by way of greeting even before Rob replied that sales were down and he didn't think advertising did a bit of good to anyone but old Catherine and her retirement account.

"That's just silly, Rob, and you know it," she retorted smartly. "You know as well as I do that she's never going to retire." Shelby perched lightly on the three-legged stool. She had deftly opened her paisley binder to a fresh page in the notebook within. She shifted to look at Riley, "I'll wait while you two finish up" she announced cheerily. Then turned to her notebook and started writing. Or doodling.

While Rob recorded the charges for Southside Industries, Riley moved closer to Shelby and asked, "How are you doing on the proposals for the shop?" She glanced up and swallowed.

"I need to stop out today and ask Daryl a few more questions. Then I should be able to meet with him and give my proposal on Wednesday." Responding to Riley's dark glare, she rushed on. "I'm sorry, but Monday and Tuesday are out because we print the paper on Tuesday. It'll be Wednesday before I can meet with him."

There it was again – she was trying to avoid Riley. *She thinks you're not good enough.* Riley coldly turned away from Shelby, grabbed the merchandise and yelled a quick "Thanks, Rob" over his shoulder before he hit the door and was gone.

"I wouldn't waste my time on Daryl," Rob stated mildly. "He wouldn't spend a plugged nickel on advertising." Shelby's hand stopped midway between sweeping her hair back from her cheek and moving to pick up her pen so she could take notes for the auto parts store's next ad.

"What do you mean?" she asked slowly with a growing feeling of dread.

"Nothin'," Rob replied. "It's just that he's owned that business for maybe forty years, and I've never once seen or heard an ad for it. Don't know why he'd start now."

Shelby went through the rest of her sales calls, but Southside Industries was on her mind. Riley was on her mind. She hadn't been able to shake the image of him Wednesday night when he said he had no rights where she was concerned. He had borne a hangdog expression briefly before concealing it and turning to move through the storm to his truck. *Does he want to have rights where I'm concerned?* She shook her head, "Don't be crazy. The man can't stand you," she said to herself.

When she returned to the office, Shelby sought out her mentor. "Bobbie, is it true that Daryl has never ever purchased an ad for Southside Industries in forty years?" Shelby queried when she had a chance to speak privately with her coworker.

Bobbie looked thoughtful, and then shrugged. "Could be. I've only been here twenty years though, so you'd have to ask Catherine or Charlie if you seriously want the full forty year history."

"Then why would he suddenly want an entire business promotional plan now?" Shelby asked.

Bobbie shifted in her chair. "I don't think he does," she responded quietly.

"I don't understand," Shelby shook her head and dropped into a nearby chair. "He called and wanted someone to meet with him – me," she paused indicating herself. "Then he doesn't show up, but sends Riley instead. Now people are telling me not to waste my time because he never advertises anyway!"

"You know, people change, businesses change, theories and applications change," Bobbie said philosophically. "The situation may not be what it appears. Don't be too quick to make assumptions though," she smiled then. "Go with the flow on this. I have a feeling that something great will come of it."

"Ya think?"

"Yes, I think," Bobbie answered. "And," she said placing a hand on Shelby's forearm, "keep an open mind. Don't judge people too quickly or too harshly."

"Okay. I'll go see if I can talk to Daryl," she said glancing to the clock. Four o'clock on a Friday – she needed to hurry.

Walking into the main area of the expansive Southside Industries building, Shelby was hit by the sensation that something was different. She looked around and found Steven

Miller smiling her way. He was dirty, but instead of holey jeans and a grungy too-tight T-shirt, he wore a uniform of steel gray khakis and button down shirt with his name embroidered on it. "Good afternoon, Shelby," he called. She smiled and responded with a small wave before pointing toward Daryl's office and raising her eyebrows questioningly. "Yep, he's in there," came the cheering reply.

As she crossed the showroom toward the half-closed door to the office, she realized what was different – besides Steve's attire and attitude. The place had been cleaned and merchandise rearranged to a much better selling advantage. She reflected that the exterior had been cleaner, too. *People change, businesses change* ... Bobbie's word came to mind. Well, so far the changes are good ones.

Her rap on the door was greeted with a quick, "Yes", so Shelby pushed the door open and moved forward with a smile. "I hope you can answer ..." The words died on her lips as Shelby's mind grasped that the man behind the desk was not who she had expected.

"Where's Daryl?" she asked flatly.

"Glad to see you, too," Riley's eyes glittered, although she wasn't certain whether it was teasing she saw there or annoyance. Perhaps both.

"Where's Daryl?"

The friendliness that she had learned to expect in Riley's expression had disappeared. She was met with a neutral look from Riley. She thought of her first impression of him, less than two weeks ago. How could she have ever thought of him as average? He stood, slowly, emitting an authority today that she hadn't before noticed, or at least hadn't acknowledged.

Looking at him today she noted that power emanated from the man before her. Suddenly she felt that she had carelessly and arrogantly walked into a mountain lion's territory and was about to be punished for her recklessness. If she was as smart as a wild rabbit she would turn tail and run for cover.

"Why do you need Daryl?" he asked with an edge in his voice. "Why don't you want to talk to me?"

"To ...," Shelby began to reply, but then stopped. Confusion whipped through her as she looked around the office. She cleared her throat and started again, "About the proposal – I told you earlier that I need to ask him some questions." Her roaming eyes came back to his gaze, "Why are you being like this?"

Riley moved around the desk and toward the door. He'd had enough of Shelby dodging him and he planned to get to the bottom of her evasiveness, but not with an audience. Intending to close the door to afford some privacy for the conversation he moved toward the office entrance.

Shelby rotated as he passed her and tracked his progress. As he closed the door and turned back to face her, Shelby's heart raced, her breathing became shallow, and adrenaline coursed through her system. Riley noted that instead of her normal healthy pink, or even one of the multiple shades of blush, that her skin normally bore, she was white as an antique doll – the porcelain ones in the vintage shop uptown.

"Being like what? I just want to know why you don't want to talk to me."

Remembered images flashed in her mind. The images she kept buried. Alarm rose within her and she fought to beat down the terror. She clutched the shoulder strap on her bag, willing the memories to stop.

She closed her eyes tightly as she tried to maintain – or regain her composure. *I will not fall apart in front of this man.* She stepped back, not thinking that she would be cornered by moving farther from the door.

Riley's gaze bored into her momentarily before he sighed and relaxed his posture. He intentionally looked away, releasing her from the rising fear.

"Sorry. I get the feeling that I just scared you?" he asked quietly, glancing now to the photo of Daryl and his family that still hung on the office wall.

Shelby shook her head fiercely, "No, you didn't," came the defiant answer.

"Well, something did," he observed. "I doubt it was the chair or the desk, so it must have been me." He sighed again, and slid his right hand through his hair then down behind his neck where he massaged the muscles. Then gesturing toward Daryl's chair behind the desk, he added, "Would you let me sit down again? Then we can start over."

Shelby moved numbly toward the chair in front of the desk to let Riley pass through, but didn't sit. "I don't think so," she said, but sounded distant. "I better get back to the office." And then she made her escape.

Cadee Brystal

CHAPTER NINE

"I just don't understand," Riley finally lamented to his big brother after a great deal of prodding.

The two had headed out well before dawn Saturday to get some quality fishing in before the lake became crowded. Andrew had grown impatient with Riley's surly attitude and silence, threatening to leave him sitting there on the ice and head into town for some real company. Andrew was almost out the door of the fish house when his little brother heaved a great sigh of defeat and announced, "Okay. I guess it couldn't hurt to talk about it."

Andrew dutifully returned to the padded seat on the five gallon bucket which held three blue gills and two perch. It was going to take more fish than that to feed themselves and their parents the promised fish fry. Absently, Andrew hoped that the fish would start biting, and soon.

Andrew pulled two sodas from the packed lunch bag and handed one to his brooding brother. "Maybe you want something stronger to drink?" he teased. "Might help you relax a bit." The comment earned him a glare.

"I thought you wanted to help," Riley accused. "You know I quit drinking."

"Yep. But you need something and sitting on an iceberg isn't helping," he added. "Are you going to make me play twenty questions or are you going to enlighten me?"

Riley growled and threw another glare at his loving brother. "I just don't understand," he reiterated.

"So you said," the older brother replied patiently. "Is it animal or mineral?" he asked as a smile touched the corners of his mouth. Riley punched him in the shoulder – harder than necessary.

"Animal, you idiot," Riley retorted. "She's definitely more complex than rock!"

"Who?" Andrew asked innocently, "Mother? Mrs. Holmes? Can't see where they would be a problem to you?"

Riley groaned, shook his head and nailed his ever-loving brother in the shoulder again. "Yes, of course. I can't figure out our mother," he replied with sarcasm.

"Hey, now. Don't get snotty with me – you're the one who needs help," Andrew laughed. "So, we are going to talk – or maybe we're not going to talk – about Shelby, the newspaper nymph?" he asked with wry confidence. "Come on," he laughed again, "It's just you and me and the fish. And if you hit me again, I *will* leave you sitting out here on the ice and head over to the lodge for a while."

Riley was not now, nor had he ever been, a person who would examine his feelings too closely. Or talk about them. What had Daryl said? *There are men who go through good times while looking for a life.* "I want a life," Riley blurted. "I was just cruising along having fun for years and suddenly I realized that I want a life. A real one. A sincere one. One that matters – that means something. I want a life that leaves a positive impact behind."

Andrew scrutinized his brother, contemplating his brief but explosive speech. "This is a good thing, Riley," Andrew nodded as he spoke, as if confirming some inner suspicion. "A very good thing" he paused. "It also explains a number of changes we've seen in you."

"Great. So I'm the last to know?" Riley snorted.

"No, you knew it. You just weren't ready to talk about it," Andrew settled his hand on Riley's shoulder. "Now, how does the newspaper nymph fit into all this?"

"I don't know. I guess ..." Riley paused. "I guess she just keeps me off-balance. I try to be nice to her and she's so suspicious of me. I feel like that kid I was in school, when everyone expects me to be bad or do something stupid. She makes me feel that way again – like she expects the worst."

Riley continued to relate the incidents between himself and Shelby. The meeting and the wink, his apology, the meeting at the coffee shop, and Friday's weird encounter at Southside Industries. Andrew grunted and nodded occasionally, but offered no insight. Finally Riley concluded, "So what should I do?"

"No idea," Andrew replied with a wide grin. "But it's sure going to be fun to watch." They fell into silence.

Riley and Andrew, each of whom had their own apartments in town, met at their parents' home nine miles west of Miller's Bend for Sunday dinner. Andrew arrived with the fish fillets from yesterday's fishing excursion and Riley provided the

Snickers salad from the local deli. The men deposited their offerings in the kitchen, before moving into the living room to watch the game with their father. "What's the score?" Andrew asked.

"Vikings can't make a touchdown to save their lives," Lawrence Wheeler grunted. "Fourteen - zip, Green Bay."

"First quarter?" Riley asked and got a confirming nod in return.

"Beth!" Lawrence yelled. No response. "Beth!"

"What do you need, Dad? I'll get it," Andrew offered. Andrew had never understood his mother's willingness to be at her husband's beck and call. He had vowed that he would never expect that treatment from his own wife. If he ever had one again.

"Can't find my glasses," the elder Wheeler responded. "She's always moving my stuff around. I laid them right here on the table," he said, indicating the spot next to his chair.

"I'll check on it," Andrew said as he moved through the passageway toward the kitchen. "Hey, Mom - Dad says you hid his glasses again," he explained as he landed a gentle kiss on her cheek. "You do that just to make him talk to you, don't you?" he asked with a quick wink.

"You know me so well," Beth replied blithely. "He left them on the dining table after breakfast. They're still there if you want to grab them for the old coot," she added as the love in her voice softened the comment.

Having delivered the run-away glasses to his father, Andrew retraced his path to the kitchen. "Mom? There are six place settings at the table," he offered as a questioning statement, inviting an explanation from his mother.

"Oh, good," she acknowledged the comment. "They haven't wandered off."

"Why, Mom? Why are there six places set?" he was suspicious now. His Mom had been on a mission to marry Andrew off to some fine upstanding hometown girl since he had returned to Miller's Bend. He considered bolting as he sensed she had set up another opportunity for him to meet Miss Right. Of course, then he'd miss the fish fry. "Who did you invite?" he hedged.

"Why, dear. You've become so mistrustful," she scolded lightly. "You really need to open your eyes. Open your heart, too, while you're at it," she patted his cheek, "it's gotten kind of musty in there, I think."

"Who, Mom?" he insisted. "I may want to go home. I can pick up a burger on the way." He stepped toward the door.

"Suit yourself," she smiled sweetly. "If you prefer a grease-burger in a bag, to these fine fresh fish my boys caught just yesterday, you go right ahead and leave. Go on." Beth had a defiant glint in her eye as she arched her brows questioningly.

"Tell me who you're trying to hook me up with now, Mom, and maybe I'll stay," he countered, "but I'm not going to be blindsided by my own mother." The two regarded each other stubbornly for a moment. Andrew feared that his mother was not going to give in and reveal the identities of the mystery guests until their arrival. "The fish is burning," he added calmly as he looked past her toward the stovetop.

"No it's not," she countered still trying to stare down her older son. "Fine," Beth sighed and turned toward the stove where one pan of fish really was burning, but she wasn't about to let on that Andrew had been right. She carefully moved the pan off the burner and turned back to face him. "Mrs. Holmes. I saw her after church today and I invited her to join us for the fish fry," she confessed.

Andrew's expression was self-satisfied, "Mrs. Holmes is going to need two place settings, Mom?"

She advanced on him wielding a spatula, "No, she's bringing a guest."

"Who, Mom? Didn't I ask this about six times now?" he pressed again.

"You are so skeptical," she shook her head, feigning sadness. "How will you ever find someone to love when you are so wary of everybody?"

Andrew's temper was rising. He didn't want someone to love. He didn't want to play meaningless games. He didn't want his happiness entwined in someone else's life. He suddenly didn't want to be here any longer either. Andrew angrily snatched his coat off the hooks by the door.

"Mother, I love you, but I swear!" Mutual exasperation permeated the space between them. "I'm leaving. I'll call you later ...." The sentence trailed off as he yanked the door open and found himself face to face with Mrs. Holmes, who grinned like the Cheshire cat.

"Oh, Andrew, thank you so much for the pleasant greeting. I hadn't even knocked yet," she greeted. "May we come in?"

"Yes, of course. Where are my manners?" he offered, opening the door wider and extending a hand to steady the grandmotherly woman. "I'm afraid, I was just going ..." he said as his gaze fell on the nymph who accompanied Mrs. Holmes. Shelby. "That is, I was just going to get something from my truck. Is there anything you would like me to bring in from your car?"

Mrs. Holmes appeared quite pleased with herself, as did Beth. "No dear, you go right ahead though," she chimed. Shelby looked uncomfortably around and then toward the Jeep. Andrew wondered idly if she was going to make a break for it.

Cadee Brystal

CHAPTER TEN

Shelby tossed the pen to the desk in her apartment and groaned. Rubbing her pounding forehead, she paced to the kitchen. She decided it was time to make some tea and take a break from the numbers. She'd spent hours trying to figure out the cost estimates and budgeting position the school board was presenting for the new athletic complex and it wasn't making any sense.

She'd thrown herself into the story after dinner at the Wheeler farm with Mrs. Holmes. What a disaster! She recalled how the sweet, no, make that conniving, old lady had appeared at Shelby's apartment door with the invitation to join her for a dinner outing. Shelby had naively accepted, thinking they were headed for a restaurant. Ha!

As events unraveled, Shelby found herself seated beside Andrew, while a seething Riley glared menacingly across the table for the entire meal. It was intensely disconcerting to know that some sort of game was afoot, but not have the slightest inclination what it might be. Nor did she understand her role in it.

It had been an awkward affair - that much was true. While Riley was quietly livid, and Andrew was more friendly and hospitable than she had expected when he had flung the door open, the emotions coursing through the room were intense, but varied greatly. Among them were bafflement and confusion from Lawrence, who apparently hadn't even known there would be company for dinner. Beth was subdued as though awaiting a great tragedy, and perhaps a bit guilty as well. And Mrs. Holmes was openly troubled by Andrew's attentions toward Shelby. Which, Shelby thought sadly, brought her right back to the earlier assessment: "What a mess," she said again to herself.

To distract herself from the failure of dinner at the Wheeler's farm, she had focused on researching the proposed new athletic complex. She wasn't a numbers person, but really didn't believe it should be so difficult to understand the information before her. She needed help. Who could she call? Who could she trust? She could ask Mrs. Holmes, but decided to give the old girl the silent treatment for a few days. Well, hours anyway.

Andrew's image came to mind. He had teasingly told her that if she ever needed help with finances to give him a call, and had boldly handed over a business card. Well, technically he had said "help with *your* finances", but she was beyond splitting hairs. She needed help with the school's finances, and Andrew was a financial advisor. He would understand the information. Regarding the business card as though it might be lethal, she carefully dialed the cell phone number listed on it. "Andrew? I need you ..." she blurted when he answered. A rich baritone laugh echoed through the phone. Shelby's face flamed. Not again! Would the horrors of the day never end? "I didn't mean it like that!" She babbled as she tried to correct the situation, "For finances. I need you for finances!"

"Shelby?" he asked tentatively.

"Yes," she exhaled in exasperation. "Can I start again? I need you professionally …" *Dear Lord, I am not an idiot. Please make me stop sounding like one.*

The soft chuckle was back in her ear. "Shelby. Relax," Andrew soothed. "I take it you have some numbers you need some help with?"

"Yes!" she replied as she began to regain her composure. "It's for a story. I just can't get the information to make sense. Can you go over it with me?"

"I'd be happy to help," Andrew answered. He considered Riley's account of how Shelby had acted when she felt cornered in the office at Southside. He considered his mother's intentions when she had invited Shelby to dinner. Lastly he considered Riley's confused feelings toward Shelby. He wondered how much longer it would be before Riley figured out that he was falling for her. Andrew decided that Shelby should pick the setting for the meeting, so he quietly asked, "Do you want an appointment at the office, or do you want to go over it at lunch?"

Silence.

"Shelby?" he paused. "You asked me to help, remember?"

"I know," she stalled. An appointment would put her alone in a closed office with Andrew. A lunch meeting would look like a date to the rest of the world – the small world of Miller's Bend at least. "How about a lunch meeting? But early. Say eleven o'clock?"

"Let me check my schedule. Yes, eleven is fine," he confirmed. "I don't suppose you want me to pick you up, do you?"

"I'll meet you at … Taco Johns?" she said with some desperation. No one could possibly think a lunch at Taco Johns was a date, could they?

Shelby, with her bag draped on her right shoulder and her tray of fast-American-Mexican food, joined Andrew in a booth at 11:05 the next morning. "Sorry I'm late," she offered apologetically. "I got held up," she added unnecessarily.

Andrew rose and greeted Shelby. "No problem. I just got here myself," he offered.

Each ate as if in solitude for a few moments, then Shelby, feeling guilty spurted, "I'm sorry about dinner yesterday." Andrew regarded her silently for a moment, looking intently, and then shook his head slightly.

"No, I'm sorry. On behalf of my entire family," he said earnestly. "We all owe you an apology. You walked into a dynamic that you didn't understand. We are usually much better behaved than what you witnessed."

"No," Shelby insisted, "My presence did … well, it did something. I shouldn't have stayed."

"Let's see what you've brought for me to see," he said indicating her bag, and abruptly dropping the family issues.

Andrew went through the papers Shelby handed him. She ate and watched his expressions as they played across his face. "You know," she said after several minutes, "I'd expect a financial advisor to have a better poker face."

His eyes lifted to hers in a question that was unvoiced. "Well," she defended her statement, "I'd say that you have just experienced confusion, an epiphany or discovery of some sort, followed by more internal questions, mild disgust, more confusion, and possibly down-right anger." She sipped her soda, wiped her mouth, placed the crumpled napkin back on the tray and looked at Andrew again. "How did I do?"

"Remind me not to gamble if you're at the table," he conceded with a smile. Then focused on the papers before him again, "Where did you get these? Is it okay with you if I make copies and go through these again more deliberately at the office?"

"I'll make copies and drop them off at your office," she offered, unwilling to let the originals out of her possession.

"And how did you say you got these?" he repeated.

"I didn't say," she replied as she tucked the papers into her bag again.

Andrew's smile was wistful. He could have really liked Shelby, if it weren't for Riley, and the fact that baby brother already had it bad for the newspaper nymph. "I'll walk you out," he offered.

Riley's color rose with his temper when he saw his beloved brother escorting Shelby from the front door of Taco Johns to her Jeep. Even as he watched them in the rear view mirror, Riley could clearly see that Andrew had pressed his hand to Shelby's back as they crossed to the parking area. Andrew tucked her into the driver's seat and leaned close to say something to her. She smiled in response before closing the door and backing out of the parking space.

Incensed, Riley sat in his truck beating back the instinct to confront Andrew. *There has to be an explanation. Andrew wouldn't try to steal my woman.* The thought froze him in place. When had he started to think of Shelby as his woman?

Hours later, Riley marched into Andrew's office. Andrew's glance lingered on Riley's distorted features for a split second before he was on his feet. "Hold on brother," he cautioned. "You need to check that attitude at the door, and we can talk."

Riley's temper roiled as he paced restlessly. "How could you?!" he demanded. "After all the things I told you, how could you make a move on Shelby?" Riley clung to the rage to suppress the anguish of the betrayal by his brother.

Andrew quickly assessed the situation. He surmised that Riley must have seen him dining with Shelby, or at least heard about it through the small town grapevine. "I didn't," he asserted. "I wouldn't. And I won't."

"Ah, but you did!" Riley exclaimed moving aggressively toward his brother.

"No. I. Did. Not," Andrew reiterated very slowly while standing his ground. "You know better than that," he sighed, and ran his fingers over the folder she had just delivered. "What I did was meet her for lunch to look at some numbers Shelby was having trouble with for a story. Because she asked me to," he answered in response to the questions brewing in Riley's eyes.

"Oh, yeah," Riley snarled. "Then since lunch went so well, she came to your office for the afternoon, huh?"

Andrew nodded, "She came by to drop off copies of the documents."

"What about dinner yesterday?" Riley demanded. His anger was beginning to ebb so he could see the logic in Andrew's explanation. But his annoyance still simmered so he pushed on. "You were flirting with her Andrew! You just had to twist the knife didn't you?"

"That was …," Andrew paused. "That was very adolescent of me. It was a gut reaction to Mom pushing women at me and I wasn't really thinking about the effect on you when it started. And then when I realized how much it bothered you … well, it just got to be too much fun to let it drop."

"So you thought you could make it better by taking her on a lunch date?" Riley still fumed and paced. "I'd really like to kick your butt right about now," he growled.

The brothers glared, each challenging the other. Finally Andrew turned away. "Riley, you know in your heart that I wouldn't try to sway a girl you have an interest in," he smiled ruefully. "I don't think I'd even try to move in on a girl I was interested in anymore," he added despondently.

Andrew's change in mood cut through Riley's self-centered anguish. "Oh, Andrew," he said quietly, "I'm sorry. I can't believe I thought …" he trailed off. Andrew dropped into the chair, looking at the framed photo on the corner of his desk. An image of himself, Lucy and their daughter, Aurora, smiled at him. He felt hollow inside. He raised his haunted eyes to Riley. "They'd have been safe if she'd have stayed with me. You know that," he said melting down into the chair.

"Aurora is safe. You know Lucy won't let anything happen to her," Riley countered, thinking of the woman and child Andrew had lost to another man. Lost for no better reason than Lucy's own inability to trust him and accept the love he offered. "Lucy, on the other hand, deserves what she gets after everything she's done to you and Aurora."

Andrew had offered Lucy a lifeline four years earlier, when she'd been beaten to the point of hospitalization by her boyfriend. Fearing for the safety of Lucy and her young daughter, he had offered marriage, safety, emotional and financial security. Lucy cautiously took him up on the proposal; but never opened her heart to Andrew. While he and Aurora loved each other with total devotion and Andrew loved Lucy, or believed he did, she never reciprocated.

Lucy, with her slender figure, her coppery blond hair and angry blue eyes, having not invested herself in the marriage, had wandered. Andrew suffered through betrayal after betrayal, until she decided to move in with her latest lover who had arrived in Miller's Bend a few months ago.

"At any rate, I'm sorry I accused you. Sorrier than you know," Riley added as he kicked the client chair that faced his brother. "Let's go. We can drown our sorrows together," he added gruffly. "You're in love with a woman whose, well … you know. And I'm going crazy over one that wishes I lived two counties over," Riley complained.

"Drown our sorrows? We don't drink. Remember?" Andrew said quietly.

"Yeah, I know. Cheeseburger and fries ought to do it," he answered as the pair headed toward the door.

CHAPTER ELEVEN

Shelby silently swept the room with her gaze, mentally tallying the number of citizens in attendance at Miller's Bend School Board's second open informational meeting concerning the proposed athletic complex. The total present appeared to be nearly double that of the first meeting only a couple weeks prior. Word had spread throughout the town and county that the school board was prepared to spend $1.25 million on a new athletic complex.

As Shelby's gaze traveled the crowd, she was pleased to realize that she was able to recognize and place more and more of the faces in the community. She spotted the presidents from all three banks, the owner of the small-town mall which housed a pharmacy and three additional businesses, as well as the owners of several of the Main Street businesses and the lumber yards. It struck her that many of those present were of the generation whose children had already finished school and moved on.

Where were the community's young parents and citizens like herself, single with no children? If the board succeeded in pushing through the plan to build, those would be the residents burdened with paying the bill - at least that was Shelby's interpretation of the muddy financial report.

Shelby startled when she realized that her eyes had stopped roaming and had zeroed in on the posse of Riley, Matt and Tyler. This evening there was a fourth person seated with them and Shelby watched intently, trying to figure out who it was. The mysterious fourth man had his back toward Shelby, but seemed very familiar. Riley glanced up and seeing Shelby, offered a smile and slight wave, but no wink. His eyes darted to the other man who pivoted in his seat to also wave to Shelby. She immediately recognized him as Riley's brother, Andrew. She waved back before turning forward in her own seat.

Was it Shelby's imagination, or had Riley's expression darkened as he watched his brother greet her? Although she was thankful that the rascal hadn't winked at her tonight, she still felt her face flush slightly. She shook her head to clear the thoughts of Riley and the posse. She could stew about them later. Then pulling her binder out of the bright plum colored bag she prepared to take notes. Even though she used a recorder for the meetings, she always took notes as well.

Mrs. Fields settled into the seat next to Shelby with a cheery, "Well hello, dear. So nice that we can sit together this time."

Shelby groaned inwardly, she did not need a talker next to her while taking notes on the important meeting ahead. "Hi, Mrs. Fields. It's so nice to see you this evening," she replied politely, even as she glanced around wondering if there was another seat available. She spotted one, right next to Andrew. *That would be out of the frying pan and into the fire.*

Since this was not a regular monthly meeting of the board, there was no agenda of regular business and in a matter of minutes Arthur Jones was waxing poetic about the benefits the proposed facility would bring to the community. The man was an incredible orator, holding the audience spellbound, until Steven Miller stood up and waited to be recognized. Jones finally subsided after the man stood for more than five minutes by Shelby's calculation.

"What is it, Mr. Miller?" Jones asked with mild disdain, "We have a copious amount of information to present tonight and I don't want you sidetracking the conversation with your drivel about how the field was good enough for you when you were on the team." He glared at Miller. Miller looked at the floor and began to bend toward his chair. Shelby thought he was going to retake his seat. *How sad. How wrong that a man who wants to address the board would be cowed into retreat.*

Suddenly the members of the posse were on their feet, along with Andrew, glaring at Jones. "Let him have his say," Riley spoke with authority. The crowd hushed and tension built within the board room. "I thought this was an open meeting of a governing board," he continued, strange strength threading through his voice, "if that's the case, then the citizens have a right to be heard."

Jones drilled Riley with a stare intended to intimidate, but clearly the town's troublemaker wasn't about to submit to authority. *Years of practice defying authority finally pays off,* Shelby thought as she scribbled in her notebook.

Jones' glare returned to Miller. The man still looked unkept, but seemed more confident than he had been during the first meeting. Then Shelby noticed that he had picked up some papers when he bent toward the chair. She continued to take notes and when she glanced toward the stage, she was startled to find Jones' focus was now on her. "And what do you think you are doing, Miss Sweetin?" he demanded in a booming voice.

Confusion swept through her. *What do I think I'm doing?* "I'm … I'm taking notes, Mr. Jones," she responded, hating the slight quiver in her voice, and the reddening she knew was on her cheeks. Her hand stilled, suspended over the notebook.

"Why are you writing, when I'm not speaking?" he demanded in a voice Shelby fancied would give Zeus a run for the money.

"She's providing quality, unbiased news reporting for our fine community, Mr. Jones," came the response from behind Shelby and slightly to the left. She didn't need to turn around to know that it was Riley who had defended her when her mind had blanked under the attack. "Surely you are aware that's the responsibility of the news media, no matter the size of the community."

There was a smattering of "Yeah", "You tell him" and "Way to go" comments among the members of the audience. The support filled Shelby with a warm feeling of being appreciated, maybe even pride in the fact that people recognized her for her professional integrity. When she looked again at Jones, it was with a certain defiance that she wouldn't have dared moments before.

Jones' turned his attention back to Miller who had approached the stage. "I've decided that for the sake of the local media, anyone who wishes to address the board tonight must do so from on stage. Do you still have something to say, Mr. Miller?" The superintendent was clearly trying to intimidate the man into abandoning his opposition to the project, or at the very least abandon his desire to address the board.

"Yes, I do," Miller declared as he mounted the steps. "I'm Steven Miller," he began addressing the board. "I work at Southside Industries. I grew up here. Went to school here. I don't know whether the proposed athletic complex is the best option for the school district. But I do know that people in this town do not take well to having things forced down their throats without a good explanation."

He cleared his throat, his Adam's apple bobbing uncomfortably as he swallowed hard. Then facing the audience, he continued, "I can't be the only person who wants to know where the money will come from for this project, how much debt will you be placing on your children and your grandchildren if this goes through." A murmur rippled through the audience. He continued, building confidence, "I can't be the only person who wonders if the board couldn't decide to repair and renovate to the existing facility for half the price, or at a huge savings." The murmur repeated in the crowd. "And I can't be the only person who wonders if this proposed complex is designed to be a monument to Mr. Jones," he concluded still standing tall.

The room was filled with gasps and muted laughter. Jones grappled with Miller to regain control of the microphone, composure lost, his eyes blazed with anger and his face bloomed with ruddiness as rage over the accusation overtook him. Jones shoved Miller toward the stairs in an attempt to regain authority over the assembly.

"That will be enough!" he yelled. "This is an informational meeting and I will explain the things the board wants you to know and you all will listen!" He paused to catch his breath, "From here on out, only selected members of the audience will be called upon to speak," he declared.

"We want to hear from the board members," someone shouted from behind Shelby. A chorus of "Yeah" sounded in response.

"I'm speaking for the board members," Jones said.

"We noticed," replied an audience member. "We want to hear what they have to say!"

"I'm speaking on behalf of the board. All the members are in agreement," Jones expounded. "There's no need to waste time having six people all tell you the same thing over and over again."

"Why not let them speak? Are you afraid of what they might say?" challenged another party. "You've muzzled them!"

"We know what's best and you people need to just sit back and let us do this!" Jones yelled as he shook his finger toward the members of the crowd. His face was in full flush, his jowls quivered and he glared hatefully at those he deemed to be questioning his authority. After minutes of silence, he drew calming breaths before proceeding. "We are taking a ten minute recess," Jones declared. "When we reconvene, the police will be here to provide security."

He clicked the mic off and strode offstage leaving silence in his wake.

CHAPTER TWELVE

Shelby phoned Southside Industries Wednesday morning and learned from Steven that neither Daryl nor Riley would be available that day. Furthermore, Daryl would be unavailable the rest of the week. Did she want Riley's phone number? Her brain screamed a resounding "NO!" but her mouth answered, "Yes, please," as she resigned herself to dealing with Riley for the promotion of the firm. Steven laughed and recited the number.

Unreasonable disappointment coursed through her when she dialed the number and it went to voice mail. "This is Shelby at the Chronicle. Please call me back to set up a time we can confer regarding the promotional plan for Southside Industries," she said in a less than perky voice. After disconnecting, she stared at her phone. Then decided to save the number as a contact, just in case.

Shelby gave up trying to apply the silent treatment to Mrs. Holmes and extended the proverbial olive branch after work Wednesday. She rapped on the back door of the house, holding a bucket of fried chicken and a container of potato salad, preparing her apology. When the door opened, Mrs. Holmes' look was one of chagrin, "Oh, Shelby," she began. "I'm so sorry," they said in unison, then burst into laughter like a couple of teenagers. Mrs. Holmes welcomed Shelby inside, "I had no idea what was going on at the Wheeler's Sunday. In fact, I still don't." She frowned, "I should talk to Beth and find out." She waved her hand as if to dispel a bad smell. "Or not."

They dined in the comfort of the sitting room with the evening news on TV. They chatted about the week and Shelby confided her frustrations about the Southside Industries account. "I can't talk to Daryl," she complained. "It's as though he's dropped off the face of the earth. And Riley hasn't returned my call." *And why does that bother me?*

"Good things come to those who wait, my dear," the older lady counseled, "You mustn't try to rush things."

"Things?" Shelby echoed. "Oh, no, Mrs. Holmes, I do not want "things" between me and Riley," she shook her head adding emphasis to the statement.

"Why on earth not? He's such a nice boy," the older woman petitioned on Riley's behalf. "And any day now, he's going to be a wonderful man. And a terrific husband." She looked to the photo of her late husband on the mantle. "I can read the signs. He'll be one of the best," she said, seemingly lost in memories. Then her attention snapped back to Shelby, "Well?"

Shelby was lost, "Well, what?" Her brows drew down.

"Why wouldn't you want Riley, dear?"

"I don't want anyone," she snapped quickly. Remorse for the peevish response tapped at Shelby's conscience. She added as an explanation, "I mean I'm not looking for a husband. I'm doing fine on my own."

"Humph. He's going to return your call for sure. Don't worry about a thing," she said confidently.

"Besides, even if I was looking, which you'll recall I am not, I wouldn't set my sights on Riley Wheeler," Shelby declared.

"Sounds like he's nothing but trouble and I steer clear of trouble."

"What trouble have you had with Riley?" Mrs. Holmes was on her feet, as near to towering over Shelby as the slight old lady could possibly be. She exuded a quiet defiance – almost as though she was personally insulted. "Well? What has he done?" she demanded.

"He …," Shelby's mind raced. *What has he done? And why is Mrs. Holmes willing to defend Riley so vehemently?*

"I never took you for an idle, slack-minded gossip, Miss Sweetin," the landlord said with extreme gentleness although sparks danced in her eyes. "I rarely make such an error."

The need to defend herself rose quickly within Shelby's soul. "Well, Mrs. Fields said that he and the posse are just a bunch of troublemakers," Shelby rallied. "And she should know, having lived here all her life." She nodded firmly as though confirming the thought to herself.

"A perverse person stirs up conflict, and a gossip separates close friends," Mrs. Holmes stated as she turned her back on Shelby. "You cannot believe everything you hear, child."

"You're saying that Mrs. Fields is perverse?" Shelby countered, rising to her feet as well. She'd been raised to respect her elders, but this was ridiculous. "Mrs. Fields, a lay-leader in the church, is perverse?"

"Not in the way you are thinking, but yes, she has some shortcomings. One of them is her love of a bad story," Mrs. Holmes explained. "Perhaps we should regain our seats, and in so doing regain our dignity, before we continue this discussion," she suggested while gesturing toward the abandoned chairs.

"Now, in Proverbs the Lord tells us important lessons about gossips, perhaps you need a good read tonight," she proceeded. "We learn that the words of a gossip are like choice morsels; they go down to the inmost parts, where I believe they can do great damage."

"But it's not gossip if it's true," Shelby pointed out, still unsure why she felt attacked in this conversation. "If Riley is a troublemaker, then it's not gossip. And I would be well advised to stay away from him," Shelby concluded with vigor.

"If. If, my dear, is one of the greatest words in our language," the elder pointed out softly. "Do you know if Riley is a troublemaker after all?"

"Well, he did wink at me during a very serious meeting," she offered as evidence. Her brows drew down in concentration, trying to bring additional evidence to the surface. "And Mr. Jones said ..."

"What Mr. Jones says is rarely of importance and even less often will you find it accurate," Mrs. Holmes spat. "A gossip betrays a confidence, but a trustworthy person keeps a secret," she continued. "You need to divine who is trustworthy, before taking information to heart, dear. And when you get home, please read Proverbs, from around chapter ten to twenty or so."

"Have you come up with any great sins that Riley has perpetrated against you?" Mrs. Holmes queried when Shelby remained silent. "I thought not. Now I believe we'd best be getting on to church this evening."

"He tried to corner me in Daryl's office!" Shelby blurted, and immediately wished desperately that she hadn't commented. It was clear that Mrs. Holmes was on Riley's side in this discussion.

"Doubtful," the elder replied thoughtfully. "Perhaps you have something personal in your past that would skew your perspective?" She held up a time-wrinkled hand to stop Shelby from speaking. "I'm not asking you to tell me the tale. I'm just asking you to consider whether Riley really was intending to do you harm, or if you just had some kind of instinctive reaction based on some trauma you've suffered before coming here."

They regarded each other silently. Shelby knew that the encounter had caused flashes of her buried memories to surface. She squirmed under the pressure of Mrs. Holmes' assessment. "Very well, Mrs. Holmes," she conceded, "I will give it some thought."

The old lady moved deftly as she started clearing the table and prepared to carry the dishes to the kitchen when Shelby rose. "I'll wash up the dishes, while you freshen up, if you'd like," she offered.

"Thank you, dear, that would be lovely," wise old eyes regarded Shelby carefully. Then Mrs. Holmes found her voice once again, "Give Riley a chance. Get to know him. Even if you are not destined for any greater relationship than that of friendship, he's a worthy man. Do not let events of the past or the opinions of others take that opportunity away from you."

The remainder of the week passed quickly. Shelby had stopped out at the Southside Industries office at least four times in two days, but found neither Riley nor Daryl. And after a several rounds of phone tag, Shelby had all but given up on connecting with Riley. As she left work Friday, Shelby decided that it would be a good weekend to visit her family. She quickly packed her travel bag and a novel. She phoned her parents to notify them she was coming. She knocked on Mrs. Holmes' door to let the landlord know she would be gone until Sunday, and was on her way.

CHAPTER THIRTEEN

Shelby arrived at her childhood home in time for the traditional pizza, popcorn and a movie Friday date night. Shelby's parents, Jack and Molly Sweetin, had implemented the weekly event seventeen years earlier – the night their oldest daughter, Sarah, now 33, was stood up by a pimply-faced teen. Molly had cradled Sarah while she cried about the injustice and then Molly wisely diverted Sarah's attention with her favorite movie. The family all joined in. And so it had begun.

Now with the family all but grown, Shelby's parents still enjoyed Friday date night. One major difference marked the tradition – these days it often turned out to be a true date for the two of them who had expended so much time and energy raising children. The family included Sarah, the oldest, a successful event planner in Sioux Falls; Samuel, who worked for a rancher near Ft. Pierre; Shelby; Sally, a full-time student at the university in Brookings, and Suzanna, who was navigating through the challenges of high school.

Suzanna surged to her feet when Shelby stepped into the TV room. Shelby's youngest sister squealed as she clasped her arms around Shelby. "I didn't know you were coming home!"

Molly joined her two daughters, wrapping her arms around each of them, "Now we can start the movie," she said with a smile. Then registering Shelby's troubled expression added, "Unless you want to talk right away or need to rest?"

Shelby smiled brightly. It felt so soothing to be home again. Her family's presence was like a balm. She let the tension melt out of her shoulders, inhaled the tantalizing aroma from the pizza. Shelby shook her head, "No way. That can wait. What's the movie?" Grabbing a slice of pizza, she dropped onto the couch next to her father, where Molly had been, smacked a big kiss on his cheek and snuggled in close. "I missed you, Daddy," she sighed as the movie started.

When Shelby and Suzanna appeared in the kitchen mid-morning Saturday, their mother looked sternly at them. "You bums missed breakfast," she observed. "I suppose you want me to whip up a batch of chocolate chip pancakes now," she offered with false censure in her voice.

"Nah, we're good until lunch," Suzanna supplied. "We ate before we went out to the barn." They had risen at dawn, which this time of year in South Dakota was around eight o'clock, and gone to the heated horse barn. Bundled warmly, the pair had trekked across the yard following the snow packed curve of the driveway toward the barn and pasture. Boots crunched in unison on the snow. The first weak rays of the sun were valiantly pushing the darkness back. Shelby smiled as she watched the sky brighten with a rosy pinkness.

The family dog, a crossbred with some Sheltie and heaven only knows what else, burst from the barn to meet the sisters as they neared. "Hey, Charlie! How ya' doin?" Shelby chimed drawing him to her before he could pause by Suzanna who bent to pet him.

"Hey, you turncoat!" Suzanna exclaimed. "Shame on you for stealing his attentions," she directed toward her sister, but she smiled broadly. "I guess I can share him for a few days."

Shelby buried her hands in his thick fur and scratched the family pet lovingly. His hair color ranged from a white bib to cream, caramel, brown and tips of black on his back. Suddenly Charlie sped toward the barn, careening through the cluster of cats that braved the cold to slip out into the snow at the approach of people; after all, there could be food involved. Cats scattered and raced for cover as Charlie snipped and snapped, threatening to roll them in the snow.

Shelby regarded the barn as they neared the door. It was the luxury their Dad had managed for the family nearly twenty years prior. "With all these girls, we'll need a diversion or they'll be chasing boys all over the countryside," he had explained. With the diversionary theory in mind he had built a horse barn with an indoor riding arena and several stalls. The horses came as the children grew. And in fact, the love for horses can forestall the love of boys, but only to a point, as Jack was disappointed to learn.

This morning, the girls had taken to the backs of their favorite mounts. Shelby was on Sparky, an aging half-Arab of questionable confirmation but sound mind and ample heart. Suzanna rode Spirit, a young quarter horse, of good confirmation, questionable mind and untested heart. They moved the horses at a walk around the perimeter of the arena. "You should come home more," Suzanna proclaimed. "It's not that far home from Miller's Bend. I miss you."

Shelby didn't respond, after all, what could she say? "Mom and Dad aren't as much fun as you might think they are." The younger sister paused as if considering some great mutiny, and then added, "I might have to get a boyfriend, you know, just to liven things up around here."

"Ha! You've probably already got one and you're just looking for a way to blame me for it," Shelby countered. She moved Sparky into a trot and Spirit followed. Soon they were cantering and crisscrossing the riding area. When they tired of riding, the two quietly untacked and groomed their mounts. They slipped the horses into their stalls intending to return them to the pasture later.

"I do," Suzanna stated out of the blue as they walked toward the house. Shelby looked at her, bewilderment in her expression. "I do have a boyfriend," Suzanna continued. "He's a senior. Mom and Dad don't like the idea. They say he's too old. What about you?"

"I don't date high school seniors," Shelby said jokingly as she tried to decipher the right response. Her mind raced, wanting to shield her baby sister from the evils of the world. Suzanna glared at her sister. "Well, I don't!" Then rolling her eyes and letting out an exaggerated sigh, she added, "I'm happy for you, of course. But please be careful. I'd hate for you to be hurt."

"Thanks, Sis. But I meant do you have a boyfriend?"

"Oh. No," she replied after a moment. Suzanna was watching her carefully as they entered the kitchen.

So as the two women and the almost-woman stood talking about pancakes and lunch, Suzanna burst forth with the impressive deduction at which she had arrived, "Hey, Mom, did you know Shelby's got a boyfriend?"

Shelby felt a thrill as the image of Riley popped into her mind. She also felt the cursed blush in her cheeks. "No. I don't," she enunciated very slowly and clearly for her sister's benefit. "Boy, it sure is cold out this morning," she attempted to divert the conversation. "Any coffee? Or maybe tea?"

"I'll start some tea while you two clean up," Molly said as she turned away to hide a smile, thinking that the development of a serious boyfriend was likely the reason for her daughter's unexpected visit.

A few minutes later, the trio sat around the dining table, stirring their tea-filled China cups. Shelby could tell her mother was biding her time, trying to let Shelby spill all the information about her non-existent boyfriend. Shelby imagined him with medium height and build, but muscular, sandy brown hair, a wicked smile, and caramel-colored eyes that twinkled with mischief just before he winked or shone with roiling emotions when he felt an injustice. *Whoa! Riley is NOT my boyfriend. Probably thinks I'm nuts by now. I bet that's why he won't return my phone calls. He's probably been meeting with Vanessa from the Shopper.* Shelby gasped and clapped a hand to her mouth as though she was about to be sick.

Molly and Suzanna turned to Shelby, eyebrows raised in question. "I do not have a boyfriend," she repeated. "I have a news story that I'm trying to break. All my energy is going into my work."

Two sets of eyes, big and unblinking like a pair of owls, gazed at Shelby. "Look, don't you think I would know it if I had a boyfriend?" Shelby demanded as she glared at her little sister. "You used to be my favorite sister," she sniffed with pretended pain. "Now I'll have to pick one of the others. Unless you let this go."

"I don't think so," quipped the youngest of the siblings. "Tell us about him."

"There isn't a 'him', so drop it," Shelby countered, leveling a glare at her sister.

"There is," Suzanna stated confidently. She shifted her attention to her mother, "Could I go stay with Shelby for a few days over Christmas break?"

"Oh, for heaven's sake, Suzanna!" Shelby blurted. Her face was crimson again and Shelby felt her pulse in the tips of her ears. Her blush had definitely gone into overdrive, and she had to escape from this room – the place that was supposed to be her haven. Shelby glanced around, yanked her coat from the hook by the door and fled the house. The winter wind burned her faced and snatched teardrops from her icy blue eyes. The wind had intensified while the ladies were inside and Shelby sought shelter in the horse barn.

CHAPTER FOURTEEN

She groomed Sparky again and fed him some grain as a treat. "They don't understand. I don't understand," she lamented to the horse. Shelby glanced toward the door, making sure her family hadn't followed. "I've been working so hard," she continued confiding in her old horse. "I want them to take me seriously. I'm a reporter, you know, not some stupid little blonde bimbo." She pretended to untangle the hair of the chestnut's mane. "I listen, I take good notes, I call people and get other points of view, and I put quotes in my stories. I'm a good reporter. Very professional, too," she nodded as if to confirm her thoughts. "So there's this new athletic complex," she explained to the equine. She looked into one of his bottomless brown eyes, "That's where the high school kids will play football and run for track, you know." Unbelievably, the horse flung his nose forward as if nodding his understanding.

"So, I'm working on that story ... well, series of stories ... and the numbers don't add up. I think there's something wrong in the financial reports, but I can't find it." She scowled as a frown formed. "It is so frustrating!" She was brushing Sparky again, and moved around to his off side. Stroking his neck she continued, "So I asked Andrew to look over the papers I received. He's a financial advisor, you know." Again Sparky bobbed his head. "You do not know, you fraud! But you are a good listener." Shelby sighed deeply. "He's also Riley's brother." Shelby fell silent, but continued brushing fiercely, as though she would strip the all the dirt from the hide of her beloved horse. Sparky turned his head to look at Shelby and reached his nose toward her. He shifted his body away.

Shelby moved to stroke his velvety nose with both hands, dropping the brush into the feed pan. "Riley is … I don't know. He confuses me. I think about him all the time – well, too much of the time. But if we end up in the same place, then we end up yelling at each other. I wish we could just talk, but it's like I assume he's thinking something and I blow up; or else he assumes I'm thinking something and he blows up. Why can't we just be civil and get to know each other." She sighed again and laid her cheek against Sparky's neck. "Mrs. Holmes thinks Riley and I should be friends. Or more. But he scares me. Oh, Sparky, what should I do?"

Sparky didn't answer.

"Ask yourself if it's really Riley that scares you, or if what scares you is your own feelings," a deep male voice counseled.

Shelby ducked under Sparky's neck and hopped over to the door of the stall. "Dad? What are you doing out here? And how long have you been listening to our private conversation?" she demanded.

"Your mother sent me with some scraps for the cats," he offered innocently. "And probably to check on you."

"She would," Shelby smiled. Sometimes it was nice to be surrounded by loving family members and sometimes it was nice to be left alone. She was definitely in the wrong place if she wanted to be left alone.

Shelby took the lead rope and returned Sparky to the pasture. Jack walked the short distance to the gate beside Shelby and Sparky, leading Spirit who had also remained in his stall after the morning ride. "Do you think Sparky has a better life when he's in the stall, or when he's out in the pasture," her father queried idly as he unlatched the gate and swung it open.

"I would say he enjoys the pasture life the best," Shelby replied. "But there are times when the stall provides a better life."

"Really. How so?"

"Well he probably feels more freedom in the pasture and the other horses are there. He can run and play or scratch each other's backs, or chase flies for each other," she said. "He can lie in the sun and drink from the stream in the pasture."

"Yes, and he can eat anytime he wants to, right?" Dad added. "What about life in the stall?"

They led the horses through the open gate before Jack swung the gate closed and latched it. He stroked Spirit's neck and slipped the halter off the gelding. Turning to Shelby, he asked, "So if you know all the benefits of pasture life, why would you put Sparky back in the stall?"

Shelby had loosened the buckle on Sparky's halter and let it slip off his nose. She rubbed his neck and gazed at her father. "There are times when he's safer in the stall," she replied with a note of suspicion.

"Ah. Safety. That's a good point. But what if you decided to keep Sparky in the safety of the stall all the time – 24/7? What would happen?" Dad quizzed.

"You know what happens to a horse that is stalled all the time, Dad," she replied. "It's not good for their mind or their body. What are you getting at?" They had watched the horses trot through the snow, over to the spot where no grass grew in the summer and the snow was hard-packed in the winter. The horses circled and dropped down into the ground where they rolled vigorously. "They can't do that in a stall either," she observed as the two horses got to their feet and shook to rid their coats of dirt and snow.

"Shelby, look at me," Dad said, as he handed Spirit's halter to her. "You are a creature who has a tremendously wonderful soul, but you've put it in a stall for safe keeping, where it is suffering. You need to move it to the pasture, where it can frolic and grow and thrive. It's time to move forward."

She stared at her father. His face was reddening with the chill of the wintery air. She noted that he'd developed lines around his eyes and mouth, and she realized that right at this moment he looked incredibly wise. But youthful pride raised its head in rebellion, "You don't know anything!" she stated as she opened the gate and passed through leaving it open for him to follow. "Safety is good."

Jack closed the gate, looked heavenward and trailed behind his steaming daughter as she headed back to the barn to return the halters to their hooks. *Grant me the right words to counsel her, Lord.*

"Shelby," her father's voice stilled Shelby's jerky movements as she hung the halters. Sighing deeply she turned again to face her father. She realized that he was trying to offer her wisdom and love, and that she was repaying him by acting like a child. "Listen to me," he said taking her in his arms. "You had a rough spell after the holdup, but you're ready to really leave it behind."

"I did. I mean, I did leave it behind, Dad," She looked again to her father's face. "Why do I get all worked up when I talk to Riley? I don't react like that around anybody else I've met in Miller's Bend ..."

"Hmmm. If God brought him into your life, or you into his life, maybe there's a reason," Dad answered as if giving the idea deep consideration. He rubbed his chin thoughtfully. "Maybe it's to help you move out of the safety of the stall and back into the fullness of life in the pasture."

"What if it wasn't God who put Riley Wheeler in my path, but the devil instead? What then?" Shelby countered somewhat sadly.

"If that's the case... No, in either case, then God will help you recognize the truth." Shelby's stomach rumbled loudly then, causing her to giggle.

"I'd better see if Mom wants me to help with lunch," she offered. "And Dad? Thanks."

The day passed quickly, as did the next and Shelby found herself feeling a bit lonely when she returned to her apartment. Lonely, but with a renewed optimism.

CHAPTER FIFTEEN

Riley was dismayed. "A person would think that two people with cell phones and modern technology could connect sometime between Wednesday and Monday," he muttered to himself after leaving yet another message on her voice mail and dropping the phone into his pocket. During the weekend he had become concerned and had gone so far as to ask Mrs. Holmes about Shelby after church Sunday. She patted him on the forearm and sing-songed her answer that good things come to those who wait. Then she assured him that Shelby was fine, just a little lost, but would soon find her way. He was confused, but she explained that Shelby had gone to visit her family for the weekend.

Since the phone tag wasn't working out so well, Riley decided to take action Monday. He pushed open the massive antique door of the newspaper office and approached the counter. An ancient woman swiveled slowly in her chair, "Can I help you?"

"I need to speak to Shelby, Ma'am," he replied.

"Shelby!" the woman bellowed toward the wall separating the lobby area from the production area. Redirecting her attention to Riley, she demanded, "Why?"

"Why? She's been working on a proposal for Southside Industries. I need to see her," Riley replied. *I need to see her?*

In his mind Riley had just begun to question the phrasing, when Shelby appeared in the doorway from the production area. "Morning," he observed as she approached. With a friendly but concerned expression, she came to a stop directly across the counter from him. She leaned forward, propping her elbows on the counter and let loose one of those incredible smiles. Riley's heart raced and his mind blanked.

"Good morning, Mr. Wheeler," she beamed. "I'm so glad we finally caught up with each other." Then for the benefit of the ancient woman, she raised her voice and added, "I must have left you twenty messages."

Shelby shone with friendliness and happiness as she looked at Riley expectantly. Suddenly Riley felt as though he was a player in an onstage production, but he didn't have a clue what his lines were to be. He wasn't even sure what play he had a part in. Hoping it wouldn't turn out to be a tragedy, he tore his eyes from Shelby's cherubic countenance. His eyes flickered to the antique wall clock, confirming the lunch hour was upon them, then to the wrinkled old grand dame of the news industry in Miller's Bend, who had grown intensely interested in the exchange. His gaze landed softly back on Shelby, who regarded him with anticipation.

"Well, since we've finally found each other, I'd suggest we make good use of the opportunity," he said. "Do you have time to meet with me now … to go over the proposal, I mean." The tips of Riley's ears burned, he knew Catherine was watching intently. He also suspected that Shelby's coworkers behind the separating wall were listening with as much interest. He held his breath and waited. The antique clock clicked as the minute hand advanced to strike the hour, followed by the chime of the outdoor clock. He exhaled and offered cautiously, "We could discuss it over lunch?"

The shadow of something dark flitted through Shelby's eyes and she began to shake her head slightly. *She can't say "no".* "I've really got to get started on the promotion, so we need to go over your ideas," he offered as he felt desperation rising. "If lunch doesn't work for you, we could meet either back here or at my office this afternoon." He'd given her options so she didn't need to feel trapped.

Shelby quickly evaluated the options he had provided. Meeting here in the newspaper office was out of the question – there would be too many spectators. Meeting at Riley's office would be alright – except she had freaked out last time they had been there together. Her stomach rumbled, just then as though offering a vote in favor of the luncheon meeting. "I guess we'd better go to lunch," she declared while patting her tummy lightly. "Just let me grab my things."

She retreated behind the wall and Riley let out the breath he'd been holding. Catherine returned to her typing, and other noises resumed in the production area. It seemed that Riley and Shelby had been center stage after all.

Shelby reappeared in moments wrapped in her no-nonsense black wool winter coat, colorful knitted hat and matching scarf. The burst of color and whimsy provided by the hat and scarf offered a bewildering contrast to the refinement of the coat, with its classic cut and basic color. The giant flower imprinted on the bag she carried bobbed cheerily on her hip as she strode across the lobby to where Riley waited. It was another example of the contradictions Shelby embodied – sporting a tropical flower during winter on the northern plains.

"Nice hat," Riley commented as he reached to open the door. A blast of polar air hit Shelby and she hunched her shoulders, pulling the coat more snugly around her neck. "Thanks, my sister made it for me. The scarf too," she added. "She gets bored living at home alone with our folks, so she taught herself to knit." Riley positioned himself to be a block against the November wind that threatened to shove Shelby away from him. He placed a hand gently to her back and steered her toward his waiting pickup, which was idling and warm inside.

"Must be nice," he commented as he opened the passenger door and boosted Shelby inside.

Once he was behind the wheel Riley noted that Shelby seemed to be inspecting him. "I could tell her I need another set," a smile lit her face as she teased. "Maybe she's got something in a more manly color." Remembering how panicked Shelby had been when they were alone in his office, Riley resisted the urge to turn fully toward her. She reminded him of a wild deer – a creature of beauty, slender and delicate, intelligent and breathtaking, but ready to flee at the first hint of danger.

He angled his head toward her, returning the smile, "I'd like that. A scarf anyway, I'm not so sure the hat would fit my image." He backed out of the parking space and headed the vehicle north on Main Street. "Where would you like to dine?"

She named a family style restaurant and they were soon settled across the table from each other in a booth designed for four. After Riley flirted with the waitress, a tired-looking woman roughly the age of Shelby's mother, they placed their orders. As the woman retreated, Shelby asked, "Why do you do that?"

"Do what?" Riley asked, feeling as though he had missed something.

"Flirt with her? She's got to be old enough to be your mother," she explained. She continued to assess Riley as he considered the question. She expected a patent denial.

"I do it to cheer her up," he said. "I try to say or do something nice to everyone I encounter during the day. It's part of my penance."

"Penance?" Shelby looked confused. "You mean you've been sentenced to community service and someone is forcing you to be nice to people?"

"You know you take everything very seriously, Miss Sweetin," he said as he shifted toward the center of his seat. The waitress arrived with their beverages, beamed at Riley, and scurried away again. "People just like it when you treat them well. And it makes me feel good to brighten someone else's day."

"That's nice, but it doesn't explain the 'penance' remark. What are you trying to make up for, Mr. Wheeler, what great sin have you committed against God and man?" Shelby wondered what was wrong with her – she had decided to give Riley a chance, and here she was challenging him over … over … well, nothing really. Her face reddened as she realized that she had pushed the conversation into dangerous territory. "Never mind. I'm sorry, I shouldn't have said that."

She pulled her eyes up to meet his gaze, expecting the anger that their previous conversations had sparked, but was met instead with a look of humorous curiosity. "No harm done," he replied quietly. "I used to like to stir things up – you know harmless stuff, like loosen the caps on the salt shakers, swap the "men's" and "women's" signs on the restroom doors. Things that were annoying and attention getting. People like Shirley here, would have to clean up after me."

"So now you go out of your way to be nice to them?" Shelby concluded.

Riley nodded, "Do you think it's helping?"

He looked so forlorn, like a little boy who had taken all the cookies and now would have to forgo supper as his punishment. "Well, I'm sure it's not hurting anything. How did you get started on your trail of adolescent delinquency?" she asked with a giggle.

Riley cleared his throat and straightened in the booth, leaning back and breaking the almost intimate atmosphere of the conversation. Shelby realized that they had both been leaning forward in rapt discussion, and the course had taken a too-personal turn. "Maybe we'll talk about that another time," he said distantly.

When the food arrived, Riley poured barbecue sauce on his French fries and bit into the burger. The smell of it was enticing and Shelby's mouth watered as she watched him. Suddenly the soup and salad held no appeal. She felt heat surge in her cheeks as she realized it wasn't the burger she wanted either. Riley held her full attention, until he realized she was watching him. He grabbed a napkin and wiped his lips then took a quenching drink. "How's the soup?" he asked with laughter dancing in his eyes.

"How's your brother?" Shelby threw the question across the table before thinking through the implications. She had felt the need to distance herself after being caught gazing at Riley like some love-struck bimbo. But, tossing Andrew into the mix had likely been a huge mistake. "I'm sorry. I shouldn't have ..." she trailed off with the apology when the steely look in Riley's eyes registered. "What is it with you two?" she asked, changing track again.

"What do you mean?" Riley responded, obviously trying to hold onto his temper.

"Well clearly you love each other, but you were acting like ... some sort of barbarian that Sunday when Mrs. Holmes and I came to dinner. And just now your hackles went up the instant I mentioned his name," she pondered. "Sibling rivalry?"

The caramel-colored eyes lit with emotion as his gaze roamed over Shelby's face and she felt it like a caress. Shelby felt herself blushing again, and looked into the bowl of quickly cooling soup. "Shelby," Riley's voice was as soft as the look in his eyes had been, pulling her gaze back to his. He reached across the table and touched her hand lightly. Shelby's heart pounded a coursing pulse in her ears and her breath became shallow. Their eyes locked. "Is he my rival?" Shelby thought she should have felt terrified, but instead she felt the gate swinging open to something greater than she had experienced before.

A clatter and shouting from the kitchen jerked Shelby back to reality and she became aware that they were sitting in a very public place having a very private moment. To break the tension, she flippantly offered, "Well, not as far as I'm concerned, but ..." She couldn't finish the statement.

Riley nodded, withdrew his hand and just looked at Shelby as he finished his dinner. Shelby finished her salad and the now cold soup before opening her bag. As she began to pull samples from the binder, Riley cleared his throat, "Do we have time for this now?" he asked indicating the clock on the wall.

Shelby only had fifteen minutes before she needed to be back at work, of course the meeting would be work, but she had other things to do today. She bit her lip, "Could it wait until Wednesday?" she asked.

"Wednesday's good if you can come to my office," he offered in reply.

"That's the second time you've called it your office, instead of Daryl's," she stated. "What's going on, where is Daryl, anyway?"

"I'll explain it all Wednesday," Riley said vaguely. "Now, I'd better get you back to work before Catherine sends the cops after me for kidnapping."

Riley parked the pickup about a half block up and across the street from the newspaper office when they returned. "I'll walk you back," he offered.

"Thank you, I'll be fine. It's less than a block," she laughed. "I'll see you Wednesday," she sang out as she waved and started across the street. Riley watched her for a few seconds, feeling optimism swelling in his spirit. They had endured each other for a whole hour without fighting. That was real progress.

He was stepping toward the bank, when the scream reached him. Riley spun toward the sound in time to see Shelby lying in the snow in the street. He raced to her side, noting a black sedan speeding away. "Lie still," he commanded. "Are you hurt?" his eyes searched her face. There was snow and dirty smudges, but no scratches or blood.

"Help me up," she countered.

"Are you hurt? Did the car hit you?" his voice was more urgent. "You can't just get up if you've been hit by a car!"

"No, I jumped clear, but ..."

"What is it?" Riley quizzed, while taking Shelby's hands and pulling her to her feet. He held her to be sure she was steady. "Tell me, now."

"I think the driver was trying to run me down," she offered weakly.

Riley looked north where the car had disappeared. Fear clutched at him. What if she'd been hurt, or killed? He wrapped Shelby's slight frame in his arms protectively. In his heart he knew he had to help her. "Why?" he whispered.

"Why do I think it, or why would they do it?" she asked as a shiver rippled through her body.

"Either," he responded flatly, while his gaze remained where he had last seen the sedan. He memorized the license plate number so he could report it to the police.

"I think it may have to do with the athletic complex," she answered, as though that was a complete explanation.

"We need to call the police."

"No. We don't."

"Why not?" Riley countered. He took Shelby firmly by the shoulders and stepped her backwards to arm's length, "Why wouldn't you call the police if someone's trying to kill ... hurt you?"

"Scare me," she said with false bravado. The look she gave Riley was pleading for understanding. "I think they are just trying to scare me. There's something wrong with the project, and I'm getting close to figuring it out."

Riley was looking at Shelby as if she'd grown a second head and was speaking an alien language.

"It's okay, Riley," she said confidently. "They wouldn't really hurt me."

As Riley crushed her back into his embrace, she thought she heard him say something like, "Nobody's going to hurt you while I'm around." But then again the sound had been muffled by her hat, the strong arms around her and the wind racing past. Maybe he hadn't said anything at all.

CHAPTER SIXTEEN

"Hello?" Shelby answered her phone tentatively. The number of the incoming call was Riley's, but she wasn't at all sure that she would want to have a conversation with him after the events earlier today. She hit the mute button on the TV remote and waited.

"You alright?" came the husky inquiry.

"I'm fine. A bit stiff, but I'm fine," she replied. "Thank you, Riley."

"Just thought I would check on you. I'll bet you didn't tell anyone did you? Not even your family?" he said with an accusing softness.

"I didn't need to tell anyone," she replied. "It was nothing."

"Says you."

"Yes. Says me," she stated firmly. "And by the way, how did the police chief come to know about this incident?"

"Oh? Did he hear about it?" Riley asked with what Shelby deemed an exaggerated air of innocence.

"Indeed, he did," she replied. "It seems an eyewitness went in and gave a statement, just in case it's needed later on."

"Good. It's nice to know the town still has some fine upstanding citizens among the residents," Riley replied, giving no hint that he may have been the one in question.

"Thank you, Riley," Shelby offered a second time in a quiet, tired voice. "It was nice of you to be there to help me after the incident. And it's nice of you to check in on me now. But you needn't have involved the law."

"You're welcome," his voice was like a balm, soothing Shelby's frayed nerves. It had been quite a day after all.

"Can I take you to lunch tomorrow?" he offered.

Shelby paused, "I'm sorry, not tomorrow. I have … a meeting scheduled." When he didn't respond, she offered, "I'd like to have lunch with you again. Maybe later in the week?"

"Okay. I'll see you Wednesday to go over the proposal, right?" he answered after what seemed an eternity.

"Right, Wednesday. Then we can do lunch Thursday or Friday?" she confirmed.

"Be careful, Shelby," Riley said cautiously. "You may be into something more serious than you know."

"I will," she promised too quickly. "Good night."

"Good night."

Shelby sat in the same booth she had shared with Riley only 23 hours before looking at Andrew. "You've got to be mistaken," she whispered in a hissed tone.

He shook his head, "Mistakes are not beneficial in my line of business, Shelby. I double checked it all. Then I checked it again." Worry etched lines around Andrew's sad eyes and Shelby wondered idly at the general gloom that seemed to wrap around the man before her. Even when he was at church, there was an air of penetrating sorrow about him.

"Okay. I'm glad you are thorough. But there's still got to be a mistake." Shelby said as she glared at the papers, as if she could change the information before her. "According to this someone has embezzled more than a million dollars from the school district in the past four or five years!" she whispered wildly.

"Shh," Andrew signaled her to be quiet. "We shouldn't discuss this here." Then his eyes narrowed on her. "Who knows you have this information? I asked you before, where did you get it?"

"Different sources ..." she trailed. "Part from Mr. Jones, part from the business manager, part from the finance officer, and part from ... well, an unidentified source. Steven Miller contributed some after one of the meetings."

"Who is the unidentified source?" Andrew asked again.

"Can't say," Shelby replied, taking a huge bite of her burger to keep her mouth busy for a while.

"You can say. And you should say, at least to someone," he said looking out the window. "Maybe you could have mentioned it to the police chief after your little accident."

"Riley told you about that?" she accused. "How could he?"

Andrew shook his head, "You know small towns better than that. Do you really think Riley was the only person who knew about your mishap? He's not talking, but plenty of others are."

She gaped at Andrew. He and Riley looked enough alike that it was obvious they were brothers, but while Riley was usually happy and cheerful – busy with his penance, spreading joy far and wide – Andrew was pessimistic, expecting the worst. "Riley's not going to be happy when he hears that we had lunch together again. What do you want me to tell him?"

Shelby was at a loss. "About the story or about us?" her brows drew down. "Tell him the truth, either way."

"Okay, but he'll be on your doorstep demanding a full disclosure within about fifteen minutes of talking to me. Don't be surprised," Andrew counseled. "What are you going to do with this information?" turning the conversation, he indicated the papers before him. "You should go to the police."

She was already shaking her head before he finished speaking. "I'll wait a while," she said. "Something is still missing, and I'm going to find it."

Riley's truck was parked in front of the house when Shelby got home from work Tuesday evening. It was press day – the day the paper is printed and mailed – and Shelby had been looking forward to a relaxing evening, but her hopes soared when she spotted the blue Chevy as she'd neared her home. Riley wasn't in his truck and was nowhere to be seen; perhaps he was visiting Mrs. Holmes until Shelby arrived. Her spirits dropped a bit as she realized that there was a chance Riley wasn't there to see her at all.

Crestfallen, Shelby made her way to the entrance to her apartment and inserted the key. She turned it, but the door was already unlocked – odd. She stepped inside as she pushed the door open, and the sight that met her was dismal.

With a start she realized that someone had approached and filled the space behind her. She whirled around to face the intruder. It was Riley's form that filled the doorway as he gazed past her at the destruction in the apartment. Shelby waited for the fear of being trapped to rise within her, but it didn't come. In its place profound relief coursed through her and she threw herself toward Riley's chest. He lightly wrapped her in his arms and kissed the top of her head.

He let out a whistle, and then observed, "Either you are a horrible house keeper, or you've had a visit from the people that you insist on ticking off." A single desperate sob escaped Shelby, before she straightened and pulled away from Riley.

"Could you call 911 for me, please?" she asked as she started to move further into the room. Riley caught her arm, stopping her progress, and pulled her back. He tucked her into the crook of his left arm, as he dialed with is right hand.

Shelby was content to take shelter huddled against Riley's solid body for the minutes he spoke with the dispatcher, but was soon squirming to move away. Riley disconnected the call, returned the phone to his pocket, and put a second hand on her other shoulder, turning her to face him. "We can't go in there. You'll disturb any evidence the police may be able to find. I'll take you up to Mrs. Holmes, and then I'll wait out front for the police."

Shelby nodded woodenly and allowed herself to be ushered to Mrs. Holmes' door where the elderly landlord met them with mild surprise. Riley explained that the apartment had been broken into and the police were on the way as he passed Shelby into Mrs. Holmes' care. Shelby was escorted into the sitting room where tea and fresh sugar cookies awaited. She wondered blankly how the woman always seemed to know what would be needed.

"There, there, child," Mrs. Holmes chanted soothingly, "this is just one of life's little storms. How lucky we are that Riley happened to be here to handle things with the police." She wrapped a colorful crocheted afghan around Shelby's shoulders and slid a cup of tea closer to her. "You know, the Lord tells us that we can rely on Him to be a hiding place from the wind, a shelter from the storm, like streams of water in a dry place." Her eyes fell on the photo of her own deceased husband and her gaze softened even more. "I don't remember where that is in the Bible, but I know it's there," she continued softly. "Since the Lord can't be here in the house with us physically, he sent Riley to help us out tonight. If we're lucky, maybe he will be your shelter even longer."

Shelby wasn't entirely comforted by the idea of Riley being her shelter from the storm. After all, he tended to rile her up whenever they were together, which to her way of thinking seemed contrary to the role of being a person's shelter. Being with Riley was definitely more like being cast about on the open sea, than being nestled in a safe quiet harbor. But not feeling the mental alertness to debate the matter, she simply sat back, resting her head against the back of the love seat and closing her eyes.

Mrs. Holmes gently cared for Shelby while Riley met with the police when they arrived. Shelby was distractedly aware of the noises of people moving through her apartment below. *Is my laundry out of sight? Will they snoop through my things? Criticize my tastes and choices? What about the burglars! What did they learn that will make me an even easier target?* Panic streaked through Shelby and she lurched suddenly to her feet.

"What is it, dear?" Mrs. Holmes asked quickly putting an arm around Shelby and lowering her again to the cushion of the love seat. The kind gray eyes assessed Shelby with a Christian love. "You're alright. Riley's handling things," she offered reassuringly. "I told you he was worthy."

Shelby's mind sharpened at the mention of the specific man in her apartment. "Why was he here?" she asked.

"Why, to see you, of course," the elder responded as a frail hand wrapped in parchment-thin skin patted Shelby's hand. "He's been here to see you before, but you weren't here. This time I knew you would be home soon, so I invited him in to wait. He loves my sugar cookies as much as you do." With a wink she added, "That's another good sign."

Shelby nodded, slightly confused by the apparent ramblings of the gray-haired angel embodied before her. The nodding changed subtly and in a few seconds Shelby was shaking her head with confusion. "What do you mean, Riley's been here before?"

"Yes, dear. When he couldn't reach you on the phone he stopped by. Didn't ask about you, but I could tell that was the real reason he was here," she expounded, nodding to herself at the memory. "Then of course, he actually inquired of you after you missed church on Sunday," she said as a frown formed in her expression. "What cause does he have to worry so about you Shelby? Are you in trouble?"

"Trouble?" Shelby echoed blankly.

"Yes, dear, trouble," the grandmotherly figure was hovering again, bringing the serving plate loaded with cookies nearer to Shelby. "You know, the kind that has criminals ransacking your apartment, and trying to run you down in the street. Trouble." Keen eyes evaluated Shelby, making her squirm in discomfort.

"I think I should call my parents," she tried weakly to turn the conversation. "May I use a bedroom so I can speak privately to them? At the rate news about me travels, they may have already heard about this incident and I better reassure them that I am just fine."

Later in the evening, when the police had finished going through the apartment for evidence, Riley paced the length of the formal sitting room in Mrs. Holmes' fine Victorian house while the police spoke quietly with Shelby in one of the bedrooms. Riley's anger seethed just below the surface, threatening to break free. Mrs. Holmes, who had told the police she hadn't notice anything out of the ordinary when she had returned from a Red Hatters meeting late in the afternoon, halted Riley's progress by appearing dead-center before him.

Hands on her hips she asked with mock sternness, "Now, Mr. Wheeler, what possible good will it do to wear a path in my rug?" He looked down at the rug that was probably about 50 years old, manufactured in the days when things were made to last. He smiled inwardly, she wasn't the least bit concerned about the dratted rug.

"A diversion?" he asked with a sad smile.

"Have you called your brother?" the waif of a woman asked.

"Why would I do that?" Riley was wary of including Andrew in anything that involved Shelby.

"Well," she drew out her reply, "they are friends, I believe." She smiled sweetly before adding, "And I think you need to see them together to put your fears to rest once and for all."

"My … fears?" Riley paused and closed his eyes to regain his composure. "And what fears would those be?"

"Oh, you know, the fear that she's got just as much interest in Andrew as she has in you," the old woman was peering into his soul, and Riley trembled with the riotous emotions coursing through him.

"What if she has?" he challenged. "She makes me crazy! She's smart, creative and witty. But she's stubborn and bullheaded and wants to fight me at every turn. When I'm with her, I just want to hold her close, and when she's not, I want to go to her and make sure she's alright. But she's scared and I couldn't stand it if I do something to push her away," he moved blindly to the vintage couch and dropped onto it with an anguished sigh. There he stayed, frozen with his elbows braced on his knees and his head in his hands, eyes staring blankly at the floor, until a hand rested lightly upon his shoulder.

"I think we need to talk," a whispered voice reached his ears.

Riley looked up into Shelby's drawn expression, and nodded. "Not tonight," he said in a voice that quavered, "not tonight." He took her hand from his shoulder and tugged her down onto the couch beside him. She leaned into his solid strength and a sigh escaped from Shelby with a slight shudder. He held her close saying nothing for the longest time. She finally shifted toward Riley and searched his face, "Why are you here?"

Exhaustion was clear in his features, as he looked helplessly at the woman he suspected he was destined to love. He answered almost reverently, "God brought me here. There's no other place I could possibly be." He gently, tenderly cupped her cheek in his calloused hand and leaned closer. Shelby's heart skipped and her breath caught and something burned deep within her. Riley touched his lips to hers briefly, then pulled her close to hold her until he dared to speak.

"I'm not sure what's happening, but I'm certain God's plan includes my being close by your side, at least until you are through making enemies to get a news story," he said. It was neither an arrogant statement, nor a presumptuous one. The man simply stated what he believed to be true.

Shelby didn't even offer an argument. "You know, a week ago, I would probably would have thought that was a line, but you might be right. I might need somebody, a friend, who's got my back until I get through with this story."

He stood and pulled Shelby to her feet. As they started down the hall toward the spare bedroom, where the police had interviewed Shelby, he announced, "I'm staying here tonight." Shelby froze in mid-stride.

Riley laughed, "On the couch. I already cleared it with Mrs. Holmes." He kissed Shelby on the cheek and retreated to the sitting room.

CHAPTER SEVENTEEN

Shelby awakened with a sense of disorientation. She glanced around the room – definitely not her style. Antique furnishings and a pink floral comforter were among the first things she noted. Shelby shuddered as she recalled the previous day's events. She had suffered a near miss by a would-be hit-and-run driver followed by the break-in at her apartment by unknown persons. Once again she expected the debilitating fear to overtake her. Instead, she remembered Riley's steadfast assistance in dealing with the police, then comforting her before sending Shelby down the hall toward the bedroom.

And she recalled that he had kissed her. Even in the mental state she had been in, that kiss had embedded in her mind, maybe even in her heart. *Oh, Lord, help me see if Riley entered my life because of your influence, or not. How much trust can I put in him? And thank you, Lord, for sending him here last night.*

She thought about the disarray in her apartment and moaned. It would take all day to clean up the mess. She needed to catalog the items that were damaged and report back to the police and to the insurance agent. The police also wanted to know if anything was missing, but had been willing to wait until today for her to go through her apartment in detail.

She peeked under the covers and felt tremendous relief that she was fully clothed in yesterday's outfit. She'd been so tired when she crashed last night, that she didn't even remember falling into bed. Resigned to the notion of starting out the day wrinkled and mildly smelly, she sat up and stretched, then gasped as the pain from the Main Street incident registered. "Oh, no," she breathed as she fell back into the soft cushioning of the mattress.

A knock sounded at the door followed too quickly by the hesitant opening of the door. "Are you decent, dear?" called Mrs. Holmes' sweetest voice. She poked her head in through the opening and beamed. "Oh, good, you're up," she chimed as she scurried into the room. "I went downstairs and picked out some fresh clothes for you. My gracious you have colorful underthings," she added as sidebar to the conversation. Shelby felt her face burn in embarrassment at the thought of the police officers going through her things the previous night.

"Were they ... out in the open?" she asked timidly, throwing an arm across her eyes as she lay on her back. *Did the police see them? Did Riley see them? Oh, please tell me "no".* She was being silly and she knew it. Someone, or maybe more than one person, wanted to at least scare her and at worst kill her, and here she was worrying about propriety.

"No harm done in that department, dear, they were safely in a drawer," Mrs. Holmes smiled before her expression saddened, "I'm afraid the apartment was quite a mess though."

"What do you mean, it *was* a mess? You mean it *is* a mess. It's going to take me all day to get it in shape so I can sleep down there tonight," Shelby said as she pulled herself upright again.

"Why don't you shower and change, before you get too worked up," the undauntable landlord persisted. "I can have your breakfast ready in about a half hour if that suits you." It wasn't a question. Before Shelby pulled her thoughts together to reply, Mrs. Holmes had deposited fresh towels and the change of clothes on the bureau and disappeared down the hall.

Exhaustion had pulled at Riley as he worked through the night to clean up in the apartment and arrange Shelby's belongings. He had tried to sleep on the couch as he told Shelby he would but his mind wouldn't grant him any rest. Each time he closed his eyes and tried to relax, he would alternately see Shelby sprawled on the icy street or worse yet, imagine her inert body on a gurney being loaded into an ambulance. The first image fueled his anger; the second imagined vision terrified him.

He had tossed and turned, gotten up and paced, even raided Mrs. Holmes' fridge, but nothing helped settle his nerves. He decided around three o'clock that physical exercise might help. He peeked in on Shelby, who was sleeping peacefully before heading down to the apartment to begin the clean-up process.

Riley chastised himself for watching Shelby sleep for the few moments he had. The intimacy of watching her shook him. She was even more beautiful as she slept; no tension or wariness was evident. His gaze skimmed away from her face, following her neck down to the edge of the pink comforter, and then followed the form of her body beneath it. She was slight, almost tiny, even when compared to other women. A piercing need to protect her had rippled through him before he closed the door. He had thrown his body and mind into righting things in Shelby's apartment for the next several hours in an attempt to keep his mind off the woman sleeping peacefully in the spare room upstairs.

Thankfully, Mrs. Holmes appeared in the doorway to Shelby's apartment around 7:30 a.m. with a mug of steaming coffee – black and well brewed – which she extended toward him. "Didn't you sleep at all, young man?" she quizzed.

He smiled weakly as he reached for the mug, "Very little. You are an absolute angel, do you know that?"

When Shelby had finished her shower, dressed and called Catherine at the Chronicle office, she followed the smells of breakfast and the sounds of voices to the kitchen. "I've taken a personal day from work," she announced as she entered the small room. Shelby's heart fluttered as she turned to Riley. A blush rose in her cheeks as their eyes met. "Thank you for staying here. For being here last night when ..." she stalled out. Her mind blanked as the look of exhaustion on Riley's features registered with her. His slightly puffy eyes had bags under them and heavy lines were etched near his eyes and mouth. The sandy hair, sporting reddish tints in the morning sunshine stood in spiky disarray, and his whiskers had been ignored and were thickening. Shelby swallowed hard.

Despite the fatigue, Riley's eyes twinkled with some mischief and a smile graced his lips. "Good morning, Shelby," he replied in a rich baritone that made her nerves quiver. "You were saying?"

She could feel the burn of the blush all the way to the tips of her ears. "I was thanking you for being here when ... when things happened," she finished lamely.

"When what happened?" he taunted gently. "You can say it Shelby."

"Say what?" she replied, bristling. "And where did that nice man go who was here last night?" she asked falsely looking out the window as though searching for the missing person. "You know, the one who was caring and supportive, strong and stable, and mature." She finished the list mentally - *totally hot and a great kisser.*

Riley rose from the table abruptly and advanced toward Shelby. She was held captive by his gaze, wishing she could retreat as he approached. *You did it now – you pushed him too far.* But before Shelby could form an apology, she read his expression and saw emotions she hadn't seen before. Her mind began to wrap around the idea that this wasn't superficial. Riley actually cared what happened to her. There was an intensity in his gaze that had her breath trapped.

"Oh, for heaven's sake," Mrs. Holmes broke in startling both of the younger two, who had somehow forgotten she was present. "I've been watching you since … Well, you Riley, since the day you were baptized, and you, young lady, since you moved in here. And you are both smart people with good souls. But right now you are both being ninnies! Now sit down," she directed.

Chagrined they settled into chairs across the table from each other. Riley stared toward the window, wondering why he hadn't gone out for a steak cube basket with Tyler and Matt last night instead of going to Mrs. Holmes' place. He knew the answer was Shelby, but thought of how much more sleep he would have gotten, and that his stomach wouldn't be hollow now if he been with the posse. *And Shelby would have had to deal with the break-in and the police alone last night.* He frowned at the thought.

Shelby had sighed heavily as she settled into the chair. Looking into the cup of coffee before her, she wondered why every conversation she and Riley had seemed destined to explode into pointless battles.

Mrs. Holmes stirred creamer into her coffee, then tapped the spoon lightly against the China cup. A light clearing of her throat drew the attention of both Shelby and Riley, who glanced briefly at each other before turning their attention respectfully to the woman they both admired. "So much pride," she said sadly. "Perhaps you've heard the old saying, pride cometh before the fall?"

Sensing this was not the time to argue, the younger two each cast their eyes downward and waited.

"Too much pride will be your downfall," she counseled. "A person needs a certain amount of pride. We use it like armor against the words and deeds of the outside world. It helps protect our spirits," she explained as she glanced from one to the other. "But you two are so full of it …," she broke off when Riley snickered, causing a giggle to break free from Shelby. Mrs. Holmes looked confused for a second before realizing that she'd just accidentally pointed out that the two were full of "it". "Well, be that as it may," she continued, "you both have an overabundance of pride. You, Riley, have used it to guard your tender, caring spirit in a world of little ruffians and authority figures who would have crushed your spirit if you had let them. And sometimes along life's way, you've even used it to take the brunt for some other person – sacrificing yourself for them."

She turned her attention to Shelby, "And you, young lady, I don't know what you've battled, but I can see that you use pride as a tool as well. At the slightest provocation, you use pride to push other people, especially Riley, back and away from yourself."

"Now look at each other," she directed. "Is the person you are looking at someone you need to guard against? Is this an enemy to your spirit? To your happiness?" She calmly sipped her coffee as she let the words settle in. "I believe God put you into each other's lives for a reason. I don't know the reason. But I'm sure that you each will benefit from the relationship if you would put down your armor when you are together."

"The Bible has several verses about the downside of pride. God encourages humility instead," Mrs. Holmes continued with barely a breath. "He tells us pride ends in humiliation, while humility brings honor," she paused. "I strongly suggest you two invest in some humility and share it with each other. Honor each other," she rose. Without another word, Mrs. Holmes placed her cup in the sink and left the room.

Riley and Shelby had been looking at each other since Mrs. Holmes commanded them to during her diatribe, and now Riley reached out to take Shelby's hand. "Wow," he whispered, "Now what?"

His stomach rumbled in response. Shelby giggled again, "Well if I dig deep for some humility, I might offer to serve you breakfast." She pulled her had free from his and moved to the stove where scrambled eggs and bacon had cooled while the two were schooled by Mrs. Holmes. Sliding a serving of each onto plates, Shelby said, "I guess we deserve a cold breakfast for our behavior." She set a plate at each place and turned to the refrigerator for drinks.

When she returned to the table, Riley had pulled her plate to the space next to his. "Would you join me for breakfast, please?" he asked with an inviting look. She nodded and settled into the chair next to his. He clasped her hand in his and bowed his head. Shelby followed suit. Then Riley prayed, asking a blessing on the food. When he finished, Shelby added, "And thank you, Lord, for the wisdom of Mrs. Holmes. And thank you for bringing Riley and me into each other's lives."

When they released each other's hands, Shelby rested her forearms on the table. "Riley, I'm sorry. I just seem to go crazy when we're together. I shouldn't have insulted you this morning."

"Apology accepted," he replied quietly. "I shouldn't have pushed you. I just wanted you to admit that you needed me. Mrs. Holmes was right; it is pride that gets us started on the road to these meaningless arguments." He was searching her eyes now and Shelby felt vulnerable and exposed. "I am sorry," he said.

"Me too," she responded. "And I did ... do need you."

CHAPTER EIGHTEEN

After breakfast, Riley offered to do dishes so Shelby could get started cleaning up in her apartment, but she insisted on helping. So they stood side by side at the double sink in Mrs. Holmes' kitchen. They didn't talk about anything of importance.

Shelby surveyed the world outside the window over the sink. The morning sun shimmered on the snow piled high by the winds. Millions of stars twinkled on the surface of the winter landscape. She was lost in thought over the story about the embezzlement. Her thoughts wound through a mental pathway, taking her on a journey through meeting with Andrew to go over the figures, lunch with Riley, and the hit-and-run attempt. She recalled his concern as he had called Monday night to check up on her. Then she remembered the deep caring he had shown last night when she discovered that her apartment had been burglarized.

Riley observed Shelby with sidelong glances as he appeared to concentrate on scrubbing the breakfast dishes. He watched her movements as she rinsed and dried the same, carefully placing them into the appropriate cupboards. It was clear that she knew her way around Mrs. Holmes' kitchen, indicating that the two had spent a great deal of time together.

Riley smiled, thinking that God had dropped another lost child into Mrs. Holmes' care, just like He had the summer when Riley himself had been on the brink of real trouble. She'd helped him find solid footing on the right path that summer, as she had helped several others in the following years.

When he finished washing, he leaned back against the counter and watched Shelby as she finished her tasks. His eyes took in her slender form. Even hidden inside the bulky sweater, he could tell she had sweet, soft curves that would be delectable to explore. He remembered holding her close the previous night as they drew fortitude from each other. He had been emotionally drained before she joined him on the couch, but when he'd kissed her, a river of new emotions had torn free and flooded his heart. His body had instinctively urged him to take the kiss and let it explode into something more. Riley's mind, however, had overridden the urge and he'd pulled back. Now as his eyes drank in the woman before him, he wondered when he would get the chance to hold her close again and kiss her once more.

A minute later, Shelby watched through the window as Riley climbed into his truck and gunned the engine. He had muttered something about needing a shower and to check in at work, but assured her he would be back with lunch by noon. After the blue Chevy truck was out of sight, Shelby headed back toward the spare bedroom, but found Mrs. Holmes reading in the sitting room. She approached the old lady slowly. "Thank you," she offered. "We needed to hear that ... I mean what you said about too much pride getting in the way," Shelby continued when her landlord looked up and met her gaze.

"That's fine, my dear," Mrs. Holmes smiled serenely. "Now what will you do?"

"I have to get started on the cleanup downstairs," Shelby replied sadly. "Do you want to come down and keep me company? You wouldn't have to help or anything ... just visit."

"I'd love to," she replied kindly, as she gently closed the book she'd been reading and placed it respectfully on the side table.

"The Bible? I thought you knew it all by heart already?" Shelby asked lightly.

"I thought I better brush up on some passages about love and passion," Mrs. Holmes answered. "I don't think you two are ready to navigate entirely on your own, and I may need some more verses to help you properly."

Shelby had no response to that statement, so she uttered an ineloquent, "Oh", as she felt the blush spread over her cheeks once again. After all, what else could she say? The woman probably had them pegged.

The two moved silently out of the main part of the house, locking it behind them. When Shelby opened the door to her apartment, she was dumbfounded. She gazed around the room which was neat and clean. Someone had picked up the items that the burglar had tossed about like an angry toddler would fling his toys. Most of Shelby's possessions had been returned to their proper places, or to places that were perfectly reasonable. A pile of items that had been broken sat in front of the couch next to boxes ready to receive them. A notebook lay nearby ready for Shelby to list the damaged items.

Shelby turned to Mrs. Holmes with questions and tears in her eyes. "Who? How?" Mrs. Holmes opened her arms to

Shelby, who slid gratefully into the hug which had been offered. "Who did this for me?" she asked again.

"Who do you think, dear?" came the quiet reply.

"Riley?" she said with a sad smile. "He must not have slept at all last night," she added.

The two spent the rest of the morning visiting while Shelby recorded in the notebook the details of the damage and tried to discover if anything had been taken. She called the police and told the chief that she would drop off the list that afternoon.

Shelby jumped when she heard a noise at the door. "Calm down, dear," Mrs. Holmes said, laying a gentle hand on her shoulder. "I'm sure it's Riley with your lunch. I'll let him in then I'll go on home."

Shelby listened to the muffled voices for a moment before Riley entered the room. A smile lit his face when he saw her sitting cross-legged on the floor studying the list in her lap. "Hi," he said.

He looked so much cleaner and fresher than he had at the breakfast table hours before. Just looking at him when she had first entered the kitchen had taken Shelby's breath away early this morning. But now she was absolutely spellbound. *I'm so lucky to have Riley in my life.* Memories of his attention and support came back to her, followed quickly by the memory of the tenderness he showed her the night before. *And that kiss!* She was mesmerized as she recalled the way he had held her, as though he never wanted to let her go. Suddenly he was directly in front of her with is hands extended. "Can I help you up?"

She set the notepad aside and clasped his hands before he quickly hoisted her to her feet and pulled her tenderly against his body. Wrapping his arms loosely around her waist, he bent to lay his rough cheek against her satiny smooth cheek. "I couldn't stop thinking about you," he whispered. After a few minutes he drew back and searched her eyes for truths that she might deny, "Are you alright?"

Nodding, she replied, "Thanks to you, I am." She stepped back, but still held onto his hands, as she glanced around the room, "I can't believe you cleaned up the whole apartment for me." She stepped closer again and her hands slid up his arms to rest on his shoulders for a second then continued their journey. As she held his face in her delicate palms, she stretched up on her toes to land a light kiss on his lips. "Thank you for everything you've done for me. And for putting up with me and my craziness."

Riley's hands had moved to Shelby's slender waist when she'd shifted closer and moved in to kiss him. When it appeared that she might start to babble, he placed the index finger of his right hand gently to her lips to silence her, while his left hand slid to the small of her back and urged her closer. He kissed her lightly once again. "You are very welcome," he whispered when their lips parted.

Then stepping back, he declared, "I wish I had known you would feel this way before I invited Andrew to join us for lunch." Raising his eyes as though looking through the ceiling to Mrs. Holmes' rooms above them, he added "We'd better join them before they eat it all." He took Shelby by the hand and led her upstairs.

Andrew and Mrs. Holmes were seated at the table talking about the high school basketball team's prospects for the season which had just begun. "Oh, good," Mrs. Holmes said, assessing the two latecomers as she scurried to the refrigerator to get drinks. Riley and Andrew had brought chicken and side dishes from the local take-out place. Riley and Shelby took their places, neither offering an explanation for their delay. Andrew grinned as he looked from one to the other then grew serious as he focused on Shelby, "I hear you've had a couple of rough days."

Shelby nodded and swallowed hard. "I think somebody's trying to scare me away from the story," she looked at Andrew but saw Riley in the periphery. He stiffened and shook his head but didn't offer comment.

An inelegant snort escaped from the normally proper Mrs. Holmes, followed by a low, "Ya think?"

The conversation reverted to the topic of local high school sports for the remainder of the meal. When everyone had eaten their fill, Shelby moved to clear the table. "I suppose you guys better be getting back to work before you get fired. I'll clean up here," she said as she moved dirty dishes to the counter by the sink. She turned back toward the table to find that no one had moved. She glanced at the clock and discovered that it was already well after one o'clock. "Oh my, you guys are already late! You had better shake a leg!"

"It's alright, Shelby, we won't get fired," Andrew said with a wink. "We have very understanding bosses."

Riley threw a strange look at his brother and added, "Everything is fine at work. They aren't expecting me back today. Besides, Mrs. Holmes has some things she wants our manly help with." He looked fondly at the grandmotherly woman seated beside him and she patted his arm.

"I'm sure lucky to have boys like you. Praise God for bringing you to my doorstep that summer," she said and she patted Riley again as though he was a little boy. "Now that's enough loafing around; we've got work to do." She looked at Shelby, "Would you mind finishing up in the kitchen while I get these two started on the next project?"

Christmas decorations were strewn about the living room when Shelby joined the others a short time later. A Nativity graced the coffee table. The pieces were arranged on an antique doily making it clear that this was the featured décor in the room. An artificial Christmas tree had been set up in one corner, but it was clearly not Mrs. Holmes' most prominent decoration. Crystal white lights twinkled on the tree, but no other decorations had been added.

"Oh good, you're just in time to help the boys put on the ornaments," Mrs. Holmes chimed. "I'll just sit back and watch the goings-on." She settled into one of the vintage chairs and watch for a moment before inspiration hit, "Andrew, would you go upstairs with me again to look for the angel for the tree top? I think we forgot her up there."

The two disappeared, leaving Riley and Shelby sorting through decorations and hanging the selected ones carefully on the tree. "This is really nice," Shelby offered.

"Hmm," Riley responded.

"I wasn't planning to decorate in my apartment, but maybe I should," she continued.

Riley didn't offer an opinion.

"Do you decorate? Oh, I suppose your mom takes care of it," she prattled, giving up on any response from the man beside her.

"Why?"

"Doesn't your mom decorate for Christmas? Mine always takes care of the decorating at home. She has us help out, but it's pretty much her baby," Shelby supplied. "I just thought maybe that was normal and that's how everybody's family does it."

"Okay, but why would you assume Mom would take care of my decorating?" Riley had stepped back from the tree and faced Shelby straight on, feet apart and his hands on his hips.

Understanding dawned on Shelby. "Uh, sorry. I assumed you still live with your folks since they are right here and all. But I'm guessing that was wrong ..."

"Yeah."

"So are you going to decorate your apartment?"

He relaxed, sighed and moved back to hanging decorations on the tree. "I'm sorry, too. I guess I was ready to overreact, huh? Yes, I do plan to decorate my place," he answered. "Would you want to come and help me sometime?"

"Sure. I'd like that a lot."

Andrew returned to the room, escorting Mrs. Holmes on his arm. The four friends continued to decorate inside the lovely Victorian house before moving outdoors to decorate the front yard. The Wheeler boys strung festive colored Christmas lights along the roofline so the house would be brightly outlined in the dark evenings before Christmas.

When they'd finished, Mrs. Holmes ordered everyone back inside for hot chocolate and treats. They readily agreed that it was time to call it a day and get warmed up again. As they sat around the small kitchen table, they discussed community events. The conversation eventually turning to the story that

Shelby was working on. Not the story about the proposed athletic complex, but the secret one that she was researching. Riley had the feeling that Andrew knew more about it than he was letting on, and Shelby was refusing to reveal any details.

Cadee Brystal

CHAPTER NINETEEN

The sweet mellow emotions of the afternoon spent decorating with Shelby, his brother and Mrs. Holmes – all people he cared about – dissolved as Riley's frustration blossomed. It wounded his pride that Shelby refused to trust him by sharing the details of her research. It wounded him even more that she apparently had entrusted those same details to his brother.

"If you tell me everything, I might be able to help figure out who's been trying to scare you off from the story," he offered, hoping the angle of trying to help would bring Shelby around to sharing the information with him. "It will be easier to keep you safe if we know who's after you," Riley said. He was shocked to hear the desperation in his own voice, and it embarrassed him to sound vulnerable.

But Shelby was shaking her head before he finished speaking. "I'm sorry Riley, but I don't think it will help and I'm just not ready to disclose the information until it I have enough proof," she said. "It's just hearsay at this point." She pleaded with him to understand, but he had turned away.

"You still don't trust me!" Riley shot the accusing statement at Shelby as he swiveled back to face her. "If you trusted me, you would tell me everything you have on these guys," he said as he glared at her across the kitchen.

Shelby's shoulders curved in a defeated posture. She let out a long sigh and replied, "You know it's not about trust, Riley. It's about ..." She shrugged. "I guess 'integrity' is the best word for it -"

A roar of anger tore from Riley, "Integrity? You're questioning my integrity?" Propelled by emotions he bolted for the exit. "I need some air," he tossed over his shoulder just before the back door slammed shut behind him.

"Do you two ever have a calm conversation?" Andrew asked Shelby. He shook his head slowly as he rose from the antique wingback chair. "I'll go talk to him."

Shelby nodded but didn't look up as Andrew left the room. "It's that stupid pride again, isn't it?"

Mrs. Holmes' appearance was one of extreme fatigue. "I'm afraid it's much more than simple pride. There are so many emotions churning around between you two that you're both very confused. And frustrated." After moving from her seat to alight next to Shelby, the elder put her arm gently around Shelby, "One day you'll figure it out. Until then – until you know in your heart – you wouldn't believe me anyway, so I'm not even going to try to explain it to you."

Shelby's mind was swirling with jumbled up thoughts and her heart was a hurricane of emotions. Mrs. Holmes was right in at least one respect she - and Riley were both victims of very intense, seemingly opposite, emotions.

"I do trust him, you know," Shelby finally offered. "I'd trust him with my life."

"Mmmm," Mrs. Holmes seemed to be digesting something distasteful, then very quietly pointed out, "With your life, you would trust him? But not with your precious story?"

Riley stood shivering near his truck several minutes before Andrew caught up with him. Adrenaline burned through his system. His heart raced and he ached to strike out – to hit something. *How can one tiny little woman make me so crazy? How can she not trust me after the last few days – the attacks and everything that's happened? How can she still question me?* A pulse pounded in his temples as he glanced at his watch. How many hours had he been without sleep? Maybe that was all he needed – sleep. Riley shook his head as another set of shivers passed over him. Sleep wasn't going to cure his insanity and he knew it. He needed Shelby, complete with her faith in him, her trust, and he suspected that he needed her love.

"You can get in and drive away, you know," Andrew said when he drew even with Riley. Dusk had fallen and with it the temperature had plummeted, but that wasn't the cause of Riley's tremors. Raw emotions and a lack of a physical outlet were brewing dangerously within him. He turned, regarding his brother carefully. "It would be easy. Just drive away. She'll be fine," Andrew taunted as the wind whipped his voice away.

"If I wanted to leave I would have," Riley said on a sigh. "I can't leave her. I can't stay with her. I can't …" he couldn't finish the statement.

Andrew thumped a palm down on Riley's shoulder. "Maybe you should just take her home –" The older brother's voice faded out as Riley's left hand streaked through the space between them to clutch his jacket front and pull him close, while the right hand poised in mid-air, as though ready to throw a punch. "Whoa, whoa, whoa! *That's* not what I meant," Andrew rushed to explain, being careful not to meet aggression with aggression.

"Just look at me!" Riley ground out as he released his brother's coat and stepped back. "Look at me! I was ready to deck you. For what? For a woman who doesn't trust me? Who doesn't care for me?" his voice had gone from a warrior's cry to a whisper as the words passed from his lips.

"If you promise not to hit me, I'll try to help," Andrew offered. The younger man nodded. "Okay. Remember – no hitting," Andrew answered himself with a smile. "Here it is: I believe you are in love, Bro."

Riley rolled his eyes and blew a breath out between clenched jaws. "Good job, Sherlock. The sky is blue, the grass is green, and baby brother's got it bad for the pretty little girl who doesn't know he's alive."

"Ohhh, she knows you're alive alright," he counseled. "She's got it just as bad as you have. The problem is … well, you know, there's more than just the one problem, but this is a big one. You two have all these very intense feelings for each other, but you've never gone on a date or had a real conversation where you can get to know each other."

"Someone is trying to hurt her – maybe they're trying to kill her – and you think we should go to the movies?" Riley asked with a tone of disbelief. "Don't you think that's a little frivolous, considering what's going on?"

"Exactly my point," Andrew replied. "You two missed the 'Hi, I'm Riley and I like ice fishing and water skiing – what do you do for fun?' stage. You went straight to the 'I'd give my life to protect you – do you think that's obsessive?' stage. You need to back it up."

"And what? You're saying we need to go on a date and talk to each other?" Riley sounded doubtful. "We can't talk to each other *with* chaperones," he said as he waived his arm toward the house indicating the recent conversation gone wrong. "What on earth do you think would happen if we were alone together?"

A wicked grin split Andrew's expression and he laughed heartily, "Well ..." The glare Riley skewered him with cut Andrew's words off before he took the thought too far.

"Trying not to think that way. You are supposed to help me figure this out," he said in exasperation.

"Okay, are you ready to listen? As I started to say, you could just take her home – to Mom and Dad's – and see if Mom could help you or Shelby, or both, navigate your way through the conversation," he offered.

Riley glared again at his brother, "Have you lost your mind?"

"You asked. If you can't talk to each other alone, then you need someone's help. Who else do you have?" he countered.

It was Riley's turn to produce a wicked grin, "You, my brother, are both a genius and the solution to my problem." Riley threw his arm around his brother's shoulders and pulled him back toward the brightly decorated house.

As they entered the sitting room from the kitchen, Riley was explaining to Andrew, "... so we'll talk and you will be my advocate, and Mrs. Holmes will be Shelby's advocate. That will keep things from getting out of control."

Andrew dug in his heels, balking in the doorway and looking at his younger brother as though he truly had lost his mind. "You better run that idea by the ladies. I think Mrs. Holmes is planning on going to the church supper and service tonight. I also think I just volunteered to be her driver," he explained as he looked around the room. "We'll be back in a couple of hours," he said as he intercepted Mrs. Holmes on her way to the door. "You kids play nice while we're gone."

The door clicked shut behind Mrs. Holmes and Andrew. An awkward silence filled the room as Riley stood staring at the door. He let out a breath and turned toward Shelby. She looked exhausted, strained and scared. The sight wrenched at something in his soul. Ruffling both hands through his hair, Riley remember the earlier lesson – humility, not pride – would be the key to the survival of their relationship. Whatever it was destined to be …

"Last night you said we need to talk. Tonight Andrew said you and I need to talk. I think we need to talk," Riley said quietly, turning a little aside. "Can I get you anything?"

Confusion and fatigue battled in Shelby's expression. She finally replied with a weak, "Yes, please. Tea would be nice. But I can get it." She started to rise, but Riley signaled her to stay.

"I'll get it. Maybe you could find a movie we would both like?" he suggested, gesturing toward the TV.

She nodded and gave him a disheartened smile. "Romantic comedy or action?" she asked. Then biting her lip, she gazed into his eyes, "I think action is the safer choice?"

"Yeah," he croaked and turned to the kitchen.

Shelby found a suitable movie on pay-per-view, Mission Impossible 4. *How many sequels can they make of a remake anyhow? And how old is Tom Cruise now?* Shelby could hear the water running in the kitchen, the clinking of cups and the hum of the microwave. Occasional muttering reached her and she smiled to herself. *Wouldn't it be nice to have a partner to share my life? He could make me tea in the evenings and we could sit around and talk. Or argue. Or fight and storm away mad. And end up hating each other.* Frowning, Shelby shook herself mentally, got up and moved down the hall.

She slipped into the bathroom to freshen up. Regarding herself in the mirror, she noted the tiredness and strain in her eyes, and the lines around her eyes which were getting puffy. She pulled out her pony tail band and let her hair fall loose. Seeing some improvement, she glanced around for a brush and quickly ran it through her locks, then flipped it to add some volume. She considered adding makeup, but decided that she wasn't on a date. Or was it? She picked up Mrs. Holmes' blush and dabbed some on and pulled the lip balm from her pocket and quickly skimmed her lips. *It's better than nothing.* She straightened her sweater and returned to the sitting room.

The aroma of buttered popcorn reached Shelby before she stepped into the room where the TV played softly. Riley stood looking out the window, which struck Shelby as very funny, since it was dark outside and he probably couldn't see anything anyhow. She looked again at the window where his reflection shown in the waves and ripples of the glass. It reminded her of a fading hologram. *What's real and what's imaginary?* Then Shelby's eye caught Riley's in the reflection and he knew she was watching him.

He turned to face her and they glided silently across the room to each other as if helpless to resist the force that captivated them. He touched her cheek gently with the backs of his fingers and searched her features with eyes that probed too deeply. She loved the rich caramel color of his eyes, but she feared that he saw too many of her secrets when he looked at her that way. She started to turn her head away from the gaze that delved into her soul.

"Please don't," he whispered. "Please don't turn away from me." It was at once a plea and a prayer, for this moment and for eternity. She raised her eyes to his and waited, feeling as though she'd laid her heart in his hands. "I'm going to kiss you," he breathed the words as he drew her close. His hands came to rest on her shoulders for only a second, and then slid up her neck to cup her face as he leaned closer. Shelby shuddered as they made contact.

Riley's mind registered Shelby's quivering response and he pulled back examining her expression, "You okay?" Shaken by her response to the complex man holding her, she nodded. "You're sure?" he asked again. Again she nodded. She closed the space between them, wrapping her arms around Riley's muscular torso and placing her head against his shoulder. He expelled a shaky breath before sliding his arms around her as well.

He closed his eyes and felt peace flood through his soul overtaking the upset and the anguish of being at odds with Shelby. He felt with certainty that he and Shelby belonged with each other. They were two pieces of a puzzle that needed to be side by side for the greater picture to make sense. God had brought them together, now it was up to them to figure out how to stick together.

"How are we going to do it, Riley," a timid voice asked after several moments had passed. The two had clung to each other, swaying gently to nonexistent music, ignoring the TV, the drinks and the popcorn. "How are we going to have a relationship without tearing each other apart?"

"I don't know. But I pledge to do everything I can to keep us together," he said as they moved to sit on the couch. He reached for the remote and clicked the movie off. "It's going to take a lot of honesty and patience."

"And humility," Shelby added as she scooted a little farther away from Riley so she could think more clearly. While they had embraced, dancing gently to the music of their souls, she had felt the assurance that being with Riley was the right choice. She had stayed quiet while they had reveled in the peace of the moment. Shelby's father's advice had come back to her. He was right, God had helped her recognize the truth – Riley's role in her life was to be a positive one. She had felt the mental gate between the stall and the lush pasture beyond swinging open, just like her father had told her. Shelby realized that she had been keeping her heart too safe, and longed to run freely in the open pasture. *Great metaphor, Dad.* She smiled to herself.

Cadee Brystal

CHAPTER TWENTY

"Do you believe God brought us together?" Riley asked as he watched Shelby who had moved not so subtly farther down the couch.

"Yes," she confirmed. "But I think it's up to us to figure out how to relate. Andrew and Mrs. Holmes have pushed us a little, but what do we do now?"

Riley considered the options then suggested, "We could pray for guidance. You know, we could use some help coming up with humility, and the ability to listen with our hearts, not just our ears."

"I think you just asked for exactly the right help," she replied.

"We need to get to know each other better. Do you want to just recite our life stories, or do you want to ask each other questions?" he offered, thinking that the reporter in Shelby, might be more comfortable steering the conversation.

She nodded, "Oh, yeah. I've got questions," she confirmed with a smile. She glanced around the room as though searching for something, "Where's my notebook?" Laughing, she turned sideways on the couch to face Riley, and then pulled her knees up to her chin. "You can start. First question?"

"Favorite color?" he fired. She frowned and he laughed, "Hey, I thought I'd start out with an easy one."

"Okay. Blue," she replied quickly.

"Then why is your bag purple with more purple?" he interjected when she would have asked a question.

"I like variety," she answered smoothly. Shelby considered which questions she most wanted answered before asking, "Why do so many people call you 'troublemaker', but I haven't seen any behavior to support that title?"

"Wow, you go right for the juggler, don't you?" Riley asked. "I don't really know how it started, maybe the frog in the teacher's desk drawer in second grade, but I do have an illustrious history of stirring things up. But that's all it ever was … just having fun and livening up society a little. I never did any real damage."

She nodded, "But why the title? And why do they still call you and the posse 'troublemakers' after all these years? It's like that's your identity or something."

"Tyler and Matt and I had fun - way too much fun - in junior high. It got to the point where the law could have been brought into it, but Mrs. Holmes got us in her clutches and straightened us out without there being an official record," he said. "I didn't want people to know that she had saved my butt." He shrugged dismissively before continuing, "She also enlightened me about God and religion. My parents are believers, but I hadn't committed myself to God until Mrs. Holmes helped me see that I needed to take that on for myself. She's been such an important influence in my life since then, too. Anyway, it wouldn't have been cool to go from a troubled teen to a goody-

goody, so I kept taking the blame for things other kids were doing to maintain my bad reputation."

"That's really stupid, Riley," Shelby offered quietly. "You quit being bad, but didn't want people to know that you had turned good?"

"Right," he confirmed. "Don't overthink it. I was a teenage boy."

"Okay."

"Well, when I did decide it was time to change my image …," he trailed off. "I guess it was too late. I went to technical school and came back, but it seemed like nobody believed that I had changed. They still judged me as a troublemaker and adolescent." He was looking toward the darkened window again.

"So you had grown up when you were a young teen, but were ashamed of the fact, so you hid it," Shelby summarized. "Then when you were ready to let the world – Miller's Bend – know that you were a responsible upstanding citizen, the town wouldn't acknowledge the fact."

"I want to be taken seriously, Shelby. I want to be respected," he said earnestly. "I've been working on that goal. That is why I was at the school board meeting where we met. I was just trying to being a good citizen. But lately, I don't care so much what anyone else thinks. Your opinion is the one that matters now. Your reactions can cut me so much deeper than other people's. It hurts so much more when you look down on me, than when the whole rest of the town does it," he said carefully. "You never knew me when I deserved to be called a troublemaker, but you still judge me as one for no reason."

"I don't judge you ..." Shelby started to refute the statement. Riley watched her face intently as she searched her mind. "I did act badly a couple of times though, and for that I'm sorry."

"You have judged me, Shelby. And you know it," he accused without rancor. Shelby realized that the man before her was so used to being mislabeled that he accepted it from most people, but that her actions had actually wounded his spirit.

"I listened to some people whom I probably shouldn't have," she allowed slowly. She looked at her hands to avoid Riley's gaze. "I listened to gossips and people who have their own agendas early on," she admitted.

She raised her eyes to Riley's face. Defeat was in his eyes and his features. She reached out toward him, but drew her hand back to rest on her knees again. "I made mistakes. But I learned. I learned not to listen to those people. I saw that you were not the rascal they portrayed. I learned to listen to my own mind - and my own heart," she spoke with gentle humility.

He didn't speak, but continued to listen intently. Defensive instincts rose within Shelby. "Well you know, you judged me without reason, too!" she tossed between them.

"No, I didn't," he said as he tensed and turned away.

"You did. You yelled at me for bringing Mrs. Holmes to church that evening," she declared.

"That wasn't judging you, Shelby," he shot back as he scrubbed his hands against his scalp. "I was concerned for her safety! You dumped an old lady off in a snowstorm for heaven's sake."

Humility. Shelby remembered that the two of them would need to bury their pride and share humility if they were going to get anywhere. After a moment, she quietly said, "You're right. It was stupid."

"What?"

"I said you're right about that night. It was stupid," she repeated.

"Oh," he replied in a bewildered tone.

"But when do you think I judged you?" she persisted. "I'm sure I didn't."

"The day you came to Southside to see Daryl," Riley countered quickly. "When you ended up in the office with me, you couldn't get away fast enough. Why did you think I wasn't worth talking to? You couldn't even spare the time of day?"

Shelby was studying her hands again as the silence stretched. *Is this the time to tell him, Lord?* She put her feet to the floor and reached for her tea. Picking it up, she discovered the cup was cold, so she placed it back on the table. Looking back to Riley, she saw defiance and a challenge in his eye. *He's daring me to deny it. Which will start a fight.* "I'm sorry, Riley, if it seemed that way to you," she began. "I can tell you that it wasn't about you that day, but it doesn't look as though you are ready to believe that, so I won't bother. But believe this, I am very sorry for the way I behaved."

Riley wanted to lash out. His instincts told him to counter, but Mrs. Holmes' words reminded him that pride would undermine the relationship with Shelby. He swallowed hard, taking a large piece of pride along, and said, "I'm sorry if I misinterpreted the situation, but it's like you sliced my heart open when you looked at me that way. I felt like you totally despised me. I've done nothing to deserve that."

Silence reigned. The clock ticked. Riley waited for the humility angle to backfire, thinking that he had just opened himself up to more criticism and judgment. *She'll think you're weak.* He opened his mouth to mount an offensive, but aborted the rising statement when she sniffled and touched his hand lightly.

"We sure are a sorry pair," she said as she gave him a watery smile. "I've hurt you without realizing it. I get so confused by you sometimes I just don't know what to do, but I'm working on it." He captured her hand in his and rubbed the back of it with his thumb.

"Are you okay to talk some more or do you want to quit?" he asked roughly.

"I'm game if you are," she replied in a chirpy tone. Her voice was too high and too cheery for the situation, but it was out there so she let it go. "Your turn to ask a question."

"Why are you taking this story about the school to the extreme that someone wants to hurt you?" he asked without a moment's thought. "Miller's Bend is a small town. The Chronicle is a small town paper. Why make waves?"

Shelby didn't think before replying, "That's what journalists do. We are the watchdogs for government. We don't just print what officials tell us to – that's what PR agents are for. We dig and find out everything they don't want you to know and then we tell you about it."

Riley was frowning. "But it doesn't matter in a small town. You go to church on Sunday and sit by Mr. Jones and then on Wednesday you print a story telling the world that he's hiding something. It doesn't work in this environment."

"It does work. Someone has been stealing money from the school district – from the taxpayers – and that needs to be exposed. I think its Jones, but I'm missing some crucial information, so I can't prove it yet," she explained with animation. "But he's scared enough to try to ..."

"Run you down in the street," Riley finished for her flatly. "Like I said, the story is not worth it."

"It's my job to report every aspect of the story, Riley," she retorted in frustration. "Why can't you get that?! I have to have the integrity to tell the whole story not just the pretty parts of it. I have to build my reputation."

"You want to be respected," he said nodding. "Just like me."

"I want people to see me as a qualified professional adult," she summarized. "Not a green kid straight out of college."

They paused to let all that they were learning about each other sink in. It seemed they both wanted the same things – to grow up and be respected. It had been an emotional twenty-four hours and now they had chosen to go over some weighted topics. Riley felt like he was drowning in the intense conversation. He needed to steer it toward easier territory, toward neutral ground.

"How about another question?" Riley suggested. "Maybe you could ask me something easy ... non-controversial."

Shelby thought carefully, searching her mind for a question that wouldn't plunge them back into deep emotional waters. Her face lit when she found the perfect query, "What's your favorite food?"

"Fish. But not from the store. I love the ones that I've caught on a lazy afternoon at a local lake. They are best when Mom cooks them up and we can sit around with the whole family together," he answered without thinking.

A frown creased her face, "That reminds me, I've been wondering what happened that Sunday? You know when Mrs. Holmes and I came to dinner at the Wheeler farm."

Riley winced, "Honestly?"

"Of course."

"Mom's been trying to set Andrew up with every single woman she knows of since … Well, anyhow, she invited Mrs. Holmes to dinner, and Mrs. Holmes invited you, right?" he paused looking to Shelby for confirmation. She nodded and indicated that he should continue.

"So Mom and Andrew got into it when he realized there were extra places set for dinner. He was about to storm out and go to the burger joint when he opened the door and found you two standing there," he laughed at the memory.

"So when Andrew was flirting with me, he was playing it up for your mom's benefit? And she was embarrassed, right?" she asked. After Riley nodded, she continued, "But what about your behavior? You were borderline barbaric."

"Well …," Riley stalled while looking very uncomfortable. A blush inched up from his neckline. He plunged forward, "Andrew and I had been fishing Saturday and we … well … I had been talking about you."

"Me?" she looked genuinely confused. "Why would you be talking about me? Men don't talk unless they have to."

He rolled his eyes, "We are slightly more evolved than that. Yes, we do talk. Sometimes."

"Okay. So you were talking about me because …" she offered to lead him back into his explanation.

He sighed and glanced at the darkened TV. "Because you confuse me. I am attracted to you, but every time we talk, we end up arguing. It's just not right. But I didn't know – I still don't know – why we do it." He looked thoughtful for a moment. "Of course, Mrs. Holmes has shed some light on the whole pride versus humility aspect. I think that may be helping," he added randomly.

Understanding dawned slowly for Shelby, "So you had spilled all of this to your brother, then the very next day he was flirting with me?" Her eyebrows shot up and her mouth formed a delightfully pleasing "Oh!" Riley nodded, looking grim. A realization hit Shelby and she continued, "And then he and I met for lunch the next day ... You must have been ..."

"Hurt? Angry? Betrayed? Yes," Riley filled in the conversational space. "And I went to talk to Andrew after work and saw you leaving his office."

"Oh, Riley. I'm sorry. I didn't know any of this," she offered as she moved closer and clasped his hand. "I would never try to hurt you. If I had known how you felt, I could have at least explained."

He was silent as he looked at the woman before him.

"But I did need to talk to him about the numbers the school district is using. That's all it was. Perfectly innocent. I've no interest in Andrew," she rushed to add.

"I know that now," he confirmed. "Now that I've seen you two together. That, and I confronted him," he added shaking his head at the memory. "Let's move forward."

Shelby had the image of the lush green pasture in her mind, "Yes," she agreed, "forward would be good. Your turn."

"You asked what happened that day at Mom and Dad's," he said as a preamble. "What I want to know is what happened that day in my office?"

"Your office?" she echoed.

"You transformed into some kind of trapped animal," he reminded her. "I thought you would claw my eyes out if I didn't give you a clear path to the door."

"I remember. But you just said 'my office'? Isn't it Daryl's office?" she watched Riley intently as the investigative reporter in her surfaced. "What's going on?"

Riley looked away briefly, then back into her face. "Ah, you don't get to ask more questions until you answer the one on the table," Riley said coolly. She fidgeted, looking at her hands and then out the window. "Shelby?"

She removed her hand from Riley's and stood. Riley let her go, sensing that she needed to collect her thoughts. She paced to the window and turned to face Riley from across the room. Distance. She had gained both emotional and physical distance, and Riley felt her rising anxiety. She drew a deep, fortifying breath, opened her mouth and closed it again. She drew a second deep breath and asked, "Do you want 'just the facts' or the whole story?"

Riley watched her carefully. She was exhausted and had been traumatized in the past few days. Between the near miss by the would-be hit-and-run driver and the burglary, she was wiped out. "If you're not up to it tonight, it's okay," he said quietly. "You can tell me another time."

She was shaking her head as she turned away. "I need to tell you, it's just that I don't know what to tell you." She stared blankly at the window again. Suddenly, she realized that Riley was standing close behind her. She felt the heat radiating off his body as they locked gazes in the reflection of the window once again.

"Your story will be safe with me," he said reassuringly. "You are safe with me." He turned her to face him. "I don't care if it's a short story or a long one, I just want to understand," he said before laying a kiss delicately on her forehead and smoothing her hair back from her face. "You are beautiful inside and out. I don't want to cause you the kind of terror I saw that day. Not ever again."

"It wasn't you," she said weakly. "Not really."

"I triggered your reaction. Something I did."

"It was silly of me," she said.

She took a deep breath and searched Riley's eyes for reassurance and found it. Reassurance and something more. What she saw in his eyes gave her the confidence to begin the story that had to be told. "Did you hear about the bank robbery in Brookings a couple years ago?" He nodded. She knew there had been a lot of TV news coverage of the blown robbery attempt and the ensuing trial, but she had deliberately avoided watching the reports, or even reading about it in the Brookings Register. She'd had enough first-hand knowledge without the news coverage.

"My friends, Allison and Ashley, and I were there that day. We were in the bank when three robbers burst through the doors," she recalled. "They looked just like normal, everyday college kids, except they wore dark clothes and masks. They were normal, everyday college kids. It turned out that Allison had dated one of the men. Somehow she recognized him and she called out his name."

Riley was afraid to move or to comment. Shelby seemed to be in a spell, watching the drama unfold in her mind. Although he hadn't known her at the time of the robbery, he was afraid for her now as she recounted the events. Clearly she was in no danger from the robbery, but fear snaked through him, urging him to try to help her. Shelby resumed her account, "He turned toward her, and he whispered her name, 'Allison'. And the fool pulled his mask off," she said. Her eyes sought Riley's again. "I watched his face as he realized what he and his friends were doing. It was like he woke up and found himself doing something that he never would have chosen to do. He dropped his gun. Just let it fall to the floor and moved toward Allison. Like he was going to embrace her – like he was coming home. And then …"

She turned away from Riley and took a couple of faltering steps. She faced him again. "I was so intent on him, that I didn't realize one of the other men had moved in behind him. He had looked so peaceful when he locked gazes with Allison, but then his face contorted in pain and he stumbled and fell. His buddy – his friend – had plunged a knife into his back. She shook her head. "There was screaming. And sirens. The robbers were trapped. We were trapped."

"Shel …," Riley stepped toward her, to offer support. "I'm so sorry, honey." She held up a hand to stop his advance.

"It's okay. I'm okay. I've told the story enough times," she said. "I can do it if I stand back."

Riley realized that as a witness, as a victim, she had been forced to recount the tale to police investigators, lawyers and others, probably dozens of times. "You don't have to go on. I get it," he offered. "Please. You don't have to go through this again."

"You deserve to know what happened. After all, whether we end up friends or in a relationship, you're going to have put up with me," she smiled warmly before retreating emotionally and resuming the story. "The police found out eventually that the guys were high, but at the time I just thought the leader had panicked. He'd stabbed his buddy in front of a room full of witnesses, one of whom knew the victim extremely well. He ordered everyone into the vaulted area, where he could lock us in. He herded us all in there – the customers and the employees. When we were all packed inside the vault, he asked which one was Allison. He had heard the other man say her name."

Riley remained frozen as he watched Shelby. His mind worked to recall any details of the bank robbery, but he wasn't coming up with much. But with Shelby telling the story from inside the action, he was beginning to share her fear as he imagined the events she now described.

"She was pregnant – Ashley and I knew it," Shelby once again sought Riley's eyes and pleaded for understanding. "She wasn't proud of it. But she accepted that she was going to be a mother. She accepted that she would have the baby to love and support and take care of. She accepted that she might have to do it alone, but she had hoped that the father might come around – that maybe he loved her enough to make a life together. Brody had been really mixed up about it … but his buddy took away all of his options that day." A tear slid down her cheek.

She shook her head again, trying to get back on track. "So the crack head ordered Allison to step forward. All three of us stepped forward. He didn't appreciate that move at all," she said with a sad laugh. "He backhanded the one closest to him, which happened to be the real Allison. She went sprawling across the cold marble floor. We dove for her to protect her."

Shelby paused as she seemed to be lost in her memories. "So there we were in a dog-pile on the floor with a drugged up maniac who wanted to kill Allison pointing a semi-automatic gun at us." Looking at Riley for reaction, she said coldly, "I was sure we were all going to be killed and I started to pray. He yelled, 'Fine. Then you all die,' and he pulled the trigger."

Riley couldn't hold himself motionless any longer, "Oh, Shelby!" he gasped as he clutched her to his chest. "You're so strong. So amazingly strong and selfless," he moaned as he rocked them back and forth soothingly. He grappled with his emotions as he silently thanked God for keeping Shelby safe through the ordeal.

"The gun jammed, Riley," Shelby said unnecessarily. "He was furious. He slammed the butt of the gun into my side. He got Ashley in the back of the head. But he didn't touch Allison. We saved her and her baby."

"The police ..." Riley stuttered as he wondered how the women had escaped further attack.

"They burst in just as he pulled the knife on us. He tried to stab a police officer before they subdued him." She shrugged as though it was nothing.

She looked up at Riley visibly returning to the present, "That day, when you slammed the door closed and turned on me, it just brought it all back. I'm sorry that I reacted the way I did."

Riley looked incredulous. "You're sorry? You're sorry that you reacted naturally to a threatening situation?" He pushed her back a step still holding her lightly by the shoulders. "I'm the one who should be sorry. And I am sorry. Now that I know some of what you've been through, I can avoid having it happen again."

"I'm sorry, I couldn't tell you sooner," Shelby said, moving closer again. "It's just not something I randomly go around telling people," she sighed as she rubbed her hands on her thighs. "Hold me?" The request was unnecessary, as Riley was already embracing her like a treasured find.

"Your friends? Are they alright?" he asked. "The baby?"

"I had broken ribs. Ashley had a concussion. Allison had a little girl six months later. Her name is Hope," she explained. "Thanks for asking about them."

"You all testified?" he asked. She nodded against his chest. "You're all still friends?"

"Thick as thieves," she confirmed.

"He's in prison?"

She nodded again, "State pen for life. The other one was sentenced for the robbery, but not for murder."

They were quiet a very long time. They moved to the couch without breaking their embrace. Reclining together, Riley tucked Shelby close against his side and vowed silently to protect her from enduring that kind of terror ever again.

That's where Andrew and Mrs. Holmes found them sound asleep when they returned from the Wednesday night church service and activities. "Looks like they worked some things through," Andrew whispered. He moved forward to awaken his brother, but a light touch on his arm stopped him.

"Let them be," she said softly.

He drew back. "What about the house rules … no sleepovers?" he asked skeptically.

"They are exhausted. Besides … I'm here to chaperone," she smiled. "Thank you for the ride to church young man. I have a good feeling about you. I think you are almost ready to open your heart again."

He rolled his shoulders and sighed. "Good night, Mrs. Holmes," he said as he headed for the door.

CHAPTER TWENTY-ONE

Riley, Andrew and Shelby arrived at the Wheeler farm for Sunday dinner with neither an invitation, nor a warning for Riley's mother. Once Beth was clear on who was dating whom, she was delighted and settled down to enjoy the visit. Shelby found Beth and Lawrence to be delightful people, although visiting them had made her long to spend time with her own family.

Shelby and Riley each spent the following weekend, Thanksgiving weekend, with their respective families. They didn't see each other for several days, and although Shelby ached to hear Riley's voice, she refused to call him. She returned to her lonely apartment Sunday evening to find a vase with an arrangement of beautiful alstroemeria, greens and baby's breath. She found a card on the table next to the flowers and paused before opening it. *Riley! Will it be a pledge of undying love?* Taking a deep breath and chastising herself for entertaining such whimsical notions, she pulled the card from the envelope. She quickly read the message, "Missed you. A lot. Supper?"

She was wiping moisture from her eyes when there was a knock at her door and a simultaneous text from Riley "I hope you're hungry because it's cold out here" it read. She sprinted to the door and flung it open to find a remarkably uncertain-looking Riley on the other side with supper in a take-out bag. "Yes!" she nearly shouted. "Oh, Riley, I'm so glad you are here."

Stepping inside and absently closing the door, he set the bag down and pulled her into his embrace. He breathed in deeply, her presence filling his senses. "I missed you," he moaned as he tightened his hold on her.

"A lot?" she quipped, turning her face up toward his. Her eyes were laughing as she added, "I missed you, too."

Then she stretched to touch her lips to his. When they stepped back, he said quietly, "Welcome home, honey."

There were no additional attacks on Shelby in the next few weeks, a fact for which Riley was extremely grateful. He and Shelby had developed the habit of meeting for lunch several days each week. They had also enjoyed many normal dates, during which they were getting to know each other better. Mrs. Holmes' recommendation to behave with humility produced excellent results in their relationship.

Sometimes, Shelby and Riley would join Matt and Tyler for supper or go together to local basketball games. She found the two men to be friendly, smart and, although Matt was a bit shy, Tyler was fun-loving and outgoing. Of course, they were all together for church services and Wednesday evening activities and were careful to include Mrs. Holmes as well. Shelby learned that the kindly old lady had helped each of the members of the posse through rough times as they were growing up.

Shelby was earning respect in the community for her newswriting and was feeling more a part of the town each day.

Although Arthur Jones complained to Catherine that Shelby's stories about the proposed athletic complex were biased against him and the project, other people would stop Shelby and tell her how much they appreciated her coverage of the issue.

Riley and Shelby had also finally gotten through the discussion in which Riley disclosed that he had purchased Southside Industries from Daryl, becoming the sole proprietor of the firm. Becoming a businessman was a point of pride for Riley, and Shelby agreed that it was a monumental step toward shaking the troublemaker image that Riley now despised. She'd been happy and supportive for him personally, and more help than he had imagined professionally. The promotional plans and suggestions she had presented were perfect for developing the business. Riley began to think of her as an integral part of the business and of his life.

By mid-December, Shelby had received a few prank calls which she attributed to misdialed numbers. She refuted Riley's insistence that someone – maybe even Jones himself – was harassing her. Riley had been concerned and called the police when she had suffered three flat tires and a broken out window within three weeks, but with no witnesses, there was no way to tie the damage to the previous hit-and-run attempt or the burglary. There had been a note in her mailbox suggesting that she needed to "Keep an eye out for strangers", which she turned over to the police at Riley's urging.

Because of his certainty that she was in danger, Shelby was reluctant to tell him when a second note appeared taped to the inside of the storm door at her apartment. She tore the note from the door and opened it slowly, reading the words "Actions that destroy lives will be returned to you". She glanced from side to side, slid it into her bag and went inside. She locked the door behind her and wondered if maybe Riley was right in believing that someone wanted to hurt her. She put the thought aside as silly – no one cared what she was doing, except maybe Jones.

She glanced at the clock. She had a covert meeting in about 15 minutes with an anonymous source who had contacted her at work claiming to have evidence about the school finances. Now she wondered if it was a trap. She looked again at the clock. Shelby was certain that if she told Riley about the note, he would try to stop her from going to the meeting. She grabbed her phone and called Andrew's number. When it rolled to voice mail, she hung up. Thirteen minutes remained. Shelby grabbed her bag and headed for her Jeep, pausing to be sure she was alone before stepping clear of the shelter of the house. She stepped up to the side of her vehicle, noticing a sheet of paper on the passenger seat, she paused again.

A shiver rattled up her spine. She knew without a doubt that there had not been anything on that seat minutes earlier. Looking around again, she pulled the door open and the interior lights came on. She checked the backseat and cargo areas for a hidden assailant. Since the Jeep was empty, she jumped inside and hit the door lock button. She carefully picked up the piece of paper and turned it over. Her breath caught when she read the words, "Revenge will be mine. Your time is running out." Shelby plunged the key into the ignition, revved the engine and slammed the Jeep into gear. She drove as her mind raced. *Who could be threatening me? Who can I turn to?* She pulled her phone out of her bag as she drove, glancing in her rear view mirror. Headlights floated menacingly behind her. Was someone following her, or was she getting paranoid?

She dialed Riley's number and waited. "Come on, come on!" she pleaded helplessly, "Pick up." The call rolled to voice mail. She tried Tyler's number with no better luck. Finally, she tried Matt's number.

"Hello," he answered cheerfully. "What's up Shelby? Looking for Riley?"

She answered somewhat distractedly, keeping one eye on the car behind her and the other eye on the road ahead. "Yeah, Matt. Do you know where he is?"

"Maybe still at the shop? I don't really know," he offered. "Is something wrong?"

"Yes. I think someone's following me," Shelby said as panic rose within her. "I don't know what to do."

"Following you?! Shelby, are you sure?" Matt asked. "Riley's going to freak!"

"Matt! Focus!" she yelled. "What do I do? I'm supposed to meet someone in five minutes, and there's a goon on my tail."

"Go to the police station," he suggested after a moment's hesitation. "If you are being followed, that should scare the guy away. I'll call the dispatcher and tell them what's going on."

Why didn't I think of that? Shelby rolled her eyes, and turned onto the street that would lead her to the police station in less than a mile. "Thanks, Matt. You're a gem," she replied. "By the way, you better let me be the one to tell Riley about this."

Shelby was flooded with relief when she spotted an officer outside the police station. She pulled into a parking space and turned to see the trailing car shoot past on the street. The officer, who had also watched the dark sedan pass, opened the door of the Jeep. "That the guy who's following you, ma'am?"

He began writing notes as Shelby replied that she believed it was.

"What else?" he asked.

Shelby looked at him blankly, "What do you mean?"

"What else is bothering you?" he asked again. "Matt called in. He said to be sure you tell me what else is going on because you wouldn't be this upset by a set of headlights in your mirror. He said there must be more to it." He watched Shelby intently, while she squirmed.

"I'm supposed to meet somebody," she said as she glanced at her watch. "I'm late and they won't wait. I really need to go."

The officer indicated that she should get out. "Come with me, please. We have paperwork to do," he said kindly.

A few minutes later Riley stormed into the room where Shelby was seated while the officer filled out forms. He looked up when Riley entered and nodded in greeting. "What happened?" Riley demanded, pausing to rest his hands on his hips and level an authoritative glare at Shelby. Relief swept through her the second she realized that he was there with her.

He was clearly worked up, and Shelby knew she shouldn't push him or he was likely to go trolling the streets in search of the vehicle that had tailed her. She stood and advanced to him, waiting for him to pull her into his embrace. "I got spooked. I'm sure it's nothing," she said with a sweet smile.

"Spooked? When you are spooked, you grab a flashlight and head toward the things that go bump in the night," he said sarcastically. "This must have scared you nearly to death to have you calling around town and speeding to the cops. So tell me what's going on."

"Matt called you," she accused as she stepped back.

"Matt, Mrs. Holmes, Tyler, and the dispatcher," he said with a slight smile. "By the way, I'm glad you're okay." He pulled her gently back into his arms for a moment.

Shelby sighed. "I'm glad you came. By the way, I did try to call you myself," she offered in her own defense. "You may as well pull up a chair, I was just about to explain everything to Officer …" she trailed off as she looked to his name tag.

"Pendleton. Josh Pendleton," the two men supplied in unison. She looked confused. "Catherine at the paper ran a story when I joined the force. It must have been just before you moved to town," the officer supplied. "It's nice to finally meet you Miss Sweetin." She nodded.

Shelby looked again to Riley, "And you know him how?"

"We are guys, Shelby," he replied with a sigh. "We hang out at the same places. He plays a mean game of pool."

Shelby and Riley sat in the institutional black chairs facing the officer's desk. The room was small and relatively new, being located in the city's community center that was built less than ten years prior. Shelby wondered if the driver of the car that had followed her was the same person who had left the notes taped to her door and resting on her passenger seat. She wondered why Jones would be taking such risky action to try to scare her. She wondered why it was working so well for him.

A shiver tripped through her slight frame as a weak sigh escaped from her lips. Suddenly, Riley's warm, work-roughened hand engulfed her smaller, soft hand. She realized then that she was cold. He rubbed her hand between his before reaching for the other hand and giving it the same treatment. "We'll do this together," he said as his gaze began to warm her. "Tell the man what's going on. I'm here for you."

Shelby was spellbound by the look in Riley's eyes. She was seeing love, devotion and possibly a lifetime together. The idea surprised Shelby and her breath caught.

The exaggerated clearing of a masculine throat brought Shelby out of her trance. She turned to look at the officer, and was aware of Riley settling back into his chair, facing forward. She glanced at him and thought he looked as though he was ready to enter the battlefield.

"Now tell me what happened," Pendleton said redirecting the conversation.

Shelby replayed the events of the evening and turned over the two notes. Riley sat silently by her side, letting the police officer lead the questioning. He would alternately rest an arm across the back of her chair, rubbing her arm occasionally, and then pull back to clasp his hands together under his chin with his elbows resting on his knees and staring at the floor.

When the officer finished listening to Shelby and asking questions, Riley leaned over to her and said calmly, "Give him the documents." Shocked, Shelby looked to Riley and shook her head. He nodded, "Yes, Shelby. It's time to turn it over to the police. Somebody is stalking you. Whether it's to scare you or hurt you, we don't know. So it's time to turn it over to the officials."

"I was supposed to get more evidence tonight," she hissed. "I was on my way to meet a source who told me he had the piece that would tie the whole thing together and then I'd be ready to bring it in. If I wait, maybe he'll contact me again, and I can still get the evidence." She looked from one man to the other.

"No Shelby, it's time now," he said firmly. "Hand it all over to the man."

Shelby hated being told what to do. She especially hated being told what to do when she could tell that the advice was sound. She knew in her heart that she was in too deep to handle the situation on her own. "I get exclusive story rights," she said to Pendleton. "I did a lot of the legwork on this and if it breaks in the regional newspaper or on the radio, I'll …" her voice trailed off. *You'll what? Threaten a police officer?* "Well, I'd like to break the story, when the time comes."

"I can't promise that, but I'll mention it to the chief," Pendleton replied. "So what's the big story you're working on?"

She huffed a little sigh of disapproval, glaring at Riley; she stalled while she tried to think of a way out of turning over her evidence. Riley shook his head again and stood as he pointed to her bag. "It's not worth getting hurt over," he said, and then added quietly, "or killed." He had turned away, but not before she read fear in his expression. The notion that he was afraid for her safety rocked Shelby.

She reached into her bag and pulled out a file of documents. "It looks like more than a million dollars has been stolen from the school district over the past four or five years," she offered as she passed the folder to the officer.

"And?" he prodded.

"And we think these documents are the reason someone is harassing Shelby," Riley directed his statement to Pendleton, but his eyes remained locked on the woman next to him. "The risk has gotten too high to continue with this story," he said. Turning his attention to the officer he added, "Now they can stalk you if they want to try to stop the theft from becoming public."

"The chief isn't going to like this," Pendleton moaned. "Where did you get all these documents, Miss Sweetin?"

"Here and there," she replied. "They are all marked with the date I received them. I've kept a record of who gave them to me." No one spoke as Pendleton flipped through the stack of documents, scowling as he did so.

"You will investigate the theft?" Shelby asked. "You won't just put it aside and forget about it, right?"

Pendleton looked insulted. "We will follow procedure, ma'am. The State's Attorney will have to review it as well."

"How soon will the key players become aware that the police have the documents, so they'll back off on harassing Shelby?" Riley inquired. "I want her kept safe until the threats stop."

"We'll increase the police presence in your neighborhood and check in with you often, until we're confident the person who has been threatening you has given up," he replied as he looked to Shelby again. "Do you have any more information?"

She shook her head, "No, I kept it all in my bag with me when I first started to think someone might be after it." A strangled sound escaped Riley's throat as he turned away, he began muttering and Shelby thought she heard something about bright people and their brilliant ideas.

"May I leave now?" she asked Pendleton cheerily.

He nodded and replied, "Yes. I've got enough here to keep me busy for the rest of my shift. Then I'll have to brief the chief when he comes in. Stay safe, Miss Sweetin. And call in if you see anything suspicious."

Riley wrapped an arm around Shelby as they left the police station and pulled her close to his side. He scanned the surroundings, feeling as though they were being watched. Shelby shivered and moved closer to his side, "I'm glad you were here for that."

"You're welcome, honey," he replied as he stopped by her Jeep and turned her to face him. "You should have left a message when you called. I could have been here sooner." He held her face in his hands, "I couldn't stand it if anything happened to you. I'd go crazy."

She pushed up onto her toes and landed a kiss on Riley's lips before dropping back on her heels. "That's sweet of you, but nothing's going to happen. The police have all the documents, so there's no reason for this guy to keep bothering me."

He pulled her door open and handed her into the Jeep. "Thanks again," she chimed and pulled the door closed. She started the engine and was just grabbing the shift lever when a blast of wintery air rolled in through the passenger door and Riley landed on the seat. "What are you doing?"

"Going with you," he replied mildly.

"No, you're not." She glared at the man beside her. "I just got rid of one stalker, I don't need another."

"You didn't get rid of him yet," Riley answered. "He's been circling the block since we came outside. I'm going with you. Now, drive."

"Oh," she answered. She backed out of the parking space and pulled onto the street. She'd only gone a few blocks when headlights appeared in her rear view again. "What about your truck?" she asked feeling defensive about being ordered around, and scared to see that Riley had been right and the man was indeed still following her.

"It's fine where it is," he replied.

"What will people think?" she said quietly. "It'll be all over town that you spent the night in jail."

"That's better than if it's parked in front of your place, Shelby," he said softly as mischief danced in his eyes. "Where would they think I spent the night then?" he challenged.

She gasped, tightening her grip on the wheel. "You are not staying the night at my place!" she yelled. Her voice was high and shaky and too loud for the small interior of the vehicle.

Riley rolled his eyes and sighed. "As much as I would like that," he replied in a voice that sent another shiver – a delicious shiver – down her spine, "I'll be staying on Mrs. Holmes' couch. And you will be in her spare bedroom. Again."

"She won't let you," Shelby challenged. She wondered just how many times she and Riley could spend the night under the same roof safely. Her mind wandered to the night they had fallen asleep together on the couch and Mrs. Holmes left them to sleep that way for the night. Some chaperone she turned out to be!

CHAPTER TWENTY-TWO

It had been two days since Shelby turned over all her research about the embezzlement to the police. They had questioned her and Riley again, as well as Andrew, as part of the official investigation. Even though Jones was now aware that the police were involved, Riley couldn't shake the uneasy feeling that the threat to Shelby was still present. He had seen that dark sedan on three more occasions while he was with Shelby. It worried him that she didn't believe she was at risk.

Riley, who had been working on a project bid for a new customer, was having trouble focusing on the plans laid before him on the desk when his cell phone buzzed. He quickly answered when he saw Shelby's name on the display, "Hello, beautiful ... I was just thinking about you," he said warmly. He was greeted by a short silence. "Shelby?"

"Hi Riley, I can't see you for lunch today. I just wanted to let you know," she said slowly, as though her mind was on something else.

His spirits plummeted. "Something's wrong?" he asked when she didn't offer an explanation.

"Kind of. I have to go out of town for a few days," she said distractedly.

"Why?"

"I'll explain when I get back," she offered.

"You're going alone?" he asked as rising concern mixed with suspicion.

"Yes."

"You're upset?"

"One of my friends, Allison. She's had … an accident. I'm going to take care of Hope for her until she's out – I mean – back on her feet again," she sounded like she really wasn't thinking clearly.

Riley's concerns were rising by the minute. "If you're upset, you shouldn't be driving." He took a deep stabilizing breath. "I could drive you, if you want me to." He waited for her reply. "Shelby?"

"Thanks, Riley, but not this time. I can do this on my own," she assured him.

"At least stop by the shop before you head out so we can say goodbye properly," he suggested, thinking that he sounded desperate. He sensed something was seriously wrong and wanted to talk to her in person to try to change her mind.

"I will," she said absently. "Bye."

He stared at the phone. *What on earth is going on?* Allison was the friend whom Shelby had been willing to sacrifice herself to save during the botched bank robbery a couple years prior. Now Shelby was dropping everything to run to her friend's aid. He wondered what had happened to Allison that she needed her friend now.

Thirty minutes later he watched as Shelby pulled out of the Southside Industries parking lot onto the highway headed for Brookings. She was alone – and so was he. She had flat out refused to allow him to go with her, or drive her or even worry about her. She insisted that she didn't need help or company and she pointed out that he had a business to run.

The explanation she'd given about Allison's accident was thin. Apparently the woman had been mugged and badly beaten. She was hospitalized and Hope was in a protective care until Shelby could get there. And she didn't want his assistance. Helplessness and loneliness ruled his emotions. He'd also been deeply disappointed that she'd refused to accept his help.

She called him a couple times while she was staying in Brookings, caring for Hope, but their conversations were awkward and far too brief. She refused to talk about Allison's attack, saying it was a fluke and that her friend was healing quickly. "Be home soon. Miss you. Bye." Riley's certainty that something was wrong grew quickly and he confided in Andrew.

Three days after Shelby had gone to her friend's aid, Riley was trying to finish some paperwork when he heard a noise. He looked up in response to register the presence of Josh Pendleton in the doorway to his office. Alarm raced through Riley as he took in the officer's stance and he shot to his feet. "What's up?" he asked cautiously.

The uniformed man looked uncomfortable. He glanced around the office, "The chief said to swing by and chat with you a minute. He said to be sure to mention the accident that's on the news," he said nodding toward the black TV screen in the corner of the tiny room. "Unofficially, of course." The man turned and was gone.

Riley looked after him for a second before jerking his attention to the TV. He grabbed the remote and thumbed it on then flipped to the local news channel. The anchor was reading a story about a freak accident where a Jeep apparently careened out of control and jumped a guardrail on a bridge over the interstate at Brookings. The driver, a 23-year-old woman, had been shaken up but was miraculously not seriously injured. Riley's heart seemed to stop. He pressed Shelby's speed dial number and was flooded with relief when she answered.

"Was it you?" he demanded. "The accident on the news – Shelby, was that you?"

She paused. "Yes, Riley, it was me," she sounded barely composed. "I don't know what happened," she choked. "I was headed home and the next thing I knew, I was spinning and crashing and falling and rolling."

"Are you okay? Are you hurt?" he asked hoarsely.

"I'm alright. They hauled me in to the hospital and checked me over," she assured him. "I was so scared, Riley."

Riley was busy thanking God for keeping the foolish woman he loved safe during the horrific accident. "I'm going to …" he began. Then thinking better of ordering Shelby around, he rephrased, "Would you like me to come and get you? I can be there in an hour." Like a man possessed, Riley had already slammed out of his office, signaled to Steven that he was leaving and pushed through the exit door. He was going to get her whether she liked it or not.

A sniffle and a sob passed through the phone, followed by a faint, "Could you?"

"Anything for you, Shelby. Don't you know I'd do anything for you?" he said as he stopped in front of his truck. "You rest until I get there."

Closing the phone, he looked at his brother who was seated behind the wheel of Riley's truck with the engine running.

Riley leveled a look intended to make his older brother cower. "What do you think you are doing?" he demanded.

"You riding or running along behind?" his brother replied as he slipped the truck into gear. "That was Shelby's Jeep in the accident on the news, right?"

Riley nodded and bolted to the passenger side. "I don't have time to argue," he said as he landed in the passenger seat, simultaneously slamming the door. "How did you know?"

"Doesn't matter," Andrew replied. A grim silence engulfed them for many miles.

When they were a few miles from Brookings, Andrew ventured, "Is she at the hospital?"

"Not sure," Riley scowled. "I'll text her."

A few minutes passed before his phone chimed. "She's at her friend's place," Riley said, then relayed the address.

As Andrew navigated the streets, he cleared his throat. "Riley," he said cautiously. "You love her, right?"

"Yeah. You know I do," he replied quietly. "What if ..."

"Riley, listen to me," he counseled, laying a gentle hand on his brother's shoulder. "You are going to want to wring her pretty little neck for scaring you like this. But if you do that, she won't forgive you. You'll scare her and push her away."

Riley glared at Andrew. His fears had transformed into anger. "Don't tell me what to do."

"Listen to me," Andrew repeated. "She needs love and support, not fear and fury." They had located the street and were nearing the apartment where Allison and Hope lived. "If you yell at her or scold her at all, she'll fight you. You could lose her."

Andrew parked the truck and the two walked purposefully toward the entrance. "I'll try," Riley finally whispered as they reached the door.

"Use your head, Riley. Remember what pride does to you two when you are together," Andrew advised as he knocked lightly.

The door opened and a slender woman with black hair and green eyes stepped back to invite them in. "Riley?" she asked belatedly.

He nodded without looking at her as his eyes swept the room for Shelby. When he located her small, still form huddled under a blanket, he went to her immediately, dropping to his knees beside the couch where she lay. He gently stroked her cheek and her eyes fluttered open.

Andrew watched for a moment before the feeling that he was intruding came over him. He turned to the woman still holding the door knob. "Yes, that's Riley," he said with a smile. "I'm his brother, Andrew," he continued and extended his hand, "you're ...?"

"Oh," the woman seemed startled. "I'm sorry. I'm Allison - Shelby's friend. Sorry, I'm kind of off base. It's been a tough few days." The stress of enduring her recent assault was evident in the bruising and the strain that shown in her features.

"No problem," Andrew offered. "Can we give them some privacy?"

Allison glanced around nervously. "Yes, we can ... We could go for a walk ..."

"How about a drive?" Andrew suggested, "You have a daughter, right?" Allison nodded in response. "I could take you two for ice cream or coffee?" Again she nodded, and moved toward the room Andrew assumed was a bedroom. She emerged moments later with a sleepy toddler bundled for a winter outing. Neither Riley nor Shelby had spoken a word, but Andrew suspected they were communicating plenty.

"Ready," she declared. As the trio departed, Andrew glanced to his brother, hoping to God that Riley wouldn't do something to mess up his love life.

Shelby had clasped Riley's hand as soon as she realized he was there. He hadn't dared speak while they had an audience. Emotions rolled through his heart and soul as he gazed sadly at the woman he loved. As soon as he heard the door close behind Andrew, Allison and Hope, he pulled Shelby into a close hug. "I was so scared," he rasped. "Will you please stop flirting with death?"

Her hands pressed against his chest. "You're all I could think about, Riley James," she admonished. "But if you just want to scold me, you may as well run after your brother and hit the road."

"You want me to leave?" he asked, as pain seared through him.

"No. I want you to love me, not scold me," she countered weakly. "I don't have the strength to fight. I just need you."

"I do love you," Riley confessed. "I thought you knew that."

She didn't answer. Andrew's advice sounded in Riley's mind, *she'll fight you and you'll lose her*. Riley sighed. "I'm sorry, Shelby."

He stood and paced, running his hands through his hair in agitation. *Just show your feelings.* "Shel, I love you and it scares me to death when things like this happen," he exclaimed. "I just don't know what to do with you!"

She slowly sat up and turned to face forward on the couch. "Come here and hold me," she suggested. "Please." She looked exhausted again, and pale. He'd missed her so much in the days she'd been gone. Now as he looked at her, she seemed so frail that wrath built fiercely in him and he struggled to hold it back. *Why does she have to endure these thing? What's happening?*

He went to her and knelt in front of her again as he had when he'd first entered the apartment. "I missed you like crazy when you left. I was hurt that you didn't want my help, but I respected you for going to your friend." He picked up her hands and held them, thinking that she felt cold. An urge to take care of her forever surged through him. "Then Pendleton showed up and said I should see the news. I flipped it on and my heart stopped when I saw the accident coverage." He paused and looked into her eyes, "Shelby, did you see the pictures of the Jeep?" She shook her head. "It's a miracle that you survived! And then you told me that you aren't even hurt. I couldn't believe it until I saw you with my own eyes."

Silent tears were streaking down her cheeks as she listened. "I'm sorry that I scared you. I don't know what happened. I can't figure it out."

"That's not important right now," he said. "I love you. I never want to lose you. I never want to spend a night wondering where you are, or if you're safe, or if and when you'll come home." He paused and closed his eyes, breathing deeply. When he opened them again, Shelby was watching him closely. He welcomed the feeling of peace and rightness that filled him. "I planned to do this on a romantic date with flowers and music and everything, but ..." he cleared his throat before continuing. "I've learned that those things aren't important. What's important is the depth of love and dedication I feel for you. I think you feel the same for me. And that we commit ourselves to each other before God and our friends."

"Riley," Shelby whispered. "I do love you. And I need you, too. But you're just talking this way because we've had a scare."

"Please, Shelby. Please marry me?" Riley asked as he pulled a velvet box from his jeans pocket. "I'm not winging it here. I love you, and I've had this for weeks. I was saving it for Christmastime. I hadn't quite figured out the details of the presentation. But I have been certain that I want to marry you for some time."

"You're sure?" she said quietly.

"Absolutely," he confirmed. He took the gold band with a simple diamond solitaire from the box.

"What about when I go nuts?" she asked, placing her hand in his.

"Even then," he said with a smile. "Even then," he repeated, as he slid the ring onto her finger.

"Oh, Riley," Shelby pulled herself forward on the couch, wincing when pain shot through her sore muscles. "I love you," She said as he stood and pulled her gently to her feet. "I'd be honored to marry you."

"Thank God," Riley whispered, just before he captured her lips in a kissed that promised their married life would be interesting, to say the least.

Cadee Brystal

CHAPTER TWENTY-THREE

Shelby returned to work Monday morning eager to get back into the quiet routine she had known before stirring up the hornet's nest of school district finances. The stress of Allison's seemingly senseless attack and the trauma of crashing her Jeep left Shelby confused and dazed. Riley's proposal seemed like a gift from God when he delivered it, but she had begun to wonder if she had accepted out of love or out of fear.

When Andrew, Allison and Hope had returned to Allison's apartment, they were excited for the newly engaged couple, but both seemed reserved about the engagement. Or maybe they were distracted about something else.

No one spoke much on the way back to Miller's Bend that day. Andrew drove while Riley cradled Shelby in the back seat of the extended cab pickup, so she could rest on the way home. Each man apparently lost in his own thoughts, as Shelby dozed. At one point, she noted that Andrew was talking on his phone, but was too tired to be curious about the conversations.

When they arrived at Shelby's apartment, Mrs. Holmes was there with homemade sugar cookies and freshly brewed tea. She efficiently settled Shelby on the couch, all the while commenting about wild drivers these days and how a girl can't be too careful. The men retreated outdoors, and Shelby raised herself up on her elbows capturing Mrs. Holmes attention. "Riley asked me to marry him," she said without preamble.

"Oh, that's wonderful, dear!" her friend nearly crowed with delight. Mrs. Holmes took on a strange glow to Shelby's mind, making her question whether she'd taken too many pain pills. "I've been praying that you two were finding your path in God's plan. Have you picked a date?"

Shelby was frowning, lost in her thoughts. She quickly jerked her head back and forth, causing pain to shoot down her neck. "No. I'm not even sure I should have accepted," she whispered peering cautiously up into Mrs. Holmes silvery gray eyes.

A quiet confidence spread through the older woman's features, "Of course you were right to accept, child. God brought you two together and I suspect he's been working very hard to keep you together." She sighed with exaggerated exasperation, "You two have been a bit of a challenge, you know. But I'm positive you are on the right road."

"How can you be so sure?"

"I just am. You need to stop questioning your love for Riley. Trust your judgment. Trust your heart. Trust God. And for heaven's sake, trust Riley. That man loves you with everything he has and everything he is."

"How do I know that what we feel truly is love? The kind of love that people can build a life on? How can I be sure?" Shelby countered weakly as she lowered herself back down onto the couch.

"You know the Bible has taught you that love is patient and love is kind. It does not envy, it does not boast, it is not proud. It is not rude, it is not self-seeking, it is not easily angered, it keeps no record of wrongs. Love does not delight in evil but rejoices with the truth. It always protects, always trusts, always hopes, always perseveres," she quoted the famous lines from Corinthians. "Does that sound like the relationship you and Riley have? I think it does."

"I think we might be a few bricks shy of a full load in a couple of those areas," Shelby said as her eyes began to drift closed. "But we are getting close."

Before she drifted into sleep, Shelby heard an angelic voice conclude softly, "Love never fails."

When she awakened, the apartment was dark. The clock read 6:18, but Shelby was disoriented. Morning? Or evening? The world outside window was dark, so no indicator there. The local news played softly on the TV, but could have been either the morning broadcast or the evening one. Stretching, Shelby pulled her aching body into a sitting position before trying to stand. She swayed and tipped precariously before starting to drop back to the couch. A strong arm wrapped suddenly and very securely around her waist. She knew instinctively that it was Riley who supported her. She leaned into his side, thankful for his presence. He never failed to be there when she needed him. *Love never fails.* The words of Mrs. Holmes returned to Shelby, she needed to trust herself and she needed to trust Riley.

"There was another note," she whispered before she realized she was even thinking it.

"I know."

"It said 'Your time is up'."

"It's not. We'll protect you, Shelby. I swear, we will keep you safe."

"How did you know?"

"Allison loves you. Apparently she knows you pretty well, too. She told Andrew about the note because she was afraid you wouldn't tell us," he replied.

"You're not upset?"

"Oh, yeah. I'm upset, alright," he said with amazing calmness. "It's just not going to help you, if you and I start fighting. So I'll just accept that you are stubborn and self-sufficient, and sometimes foolish. And I will love you anyway." He kissed her then with tenderness and devotion. The kiss morphed, taking on a life of its own, becoming an expression of passion, hopes, dreams and fears all rolled into one. When they broke away from each other, they each had to battle internally to regain their composure.

"We had better get a date set for the wedding," Riley said when he finally spoke. "Soon."

They had a light supper before Shelby was ready to crash for the night. She tried to send Riley home so she could go to bed, but he informed her that he would be guarding her that night. "You cannot stay here!" she exclaimed.

"It's going be just like the other times, Shelby. You're in the guest room upstairs, I'm on the couch and Mrs. Holmes is keeping her eye on us," he explained with frustration. "I'm going to protect you from this guy."

Who's going to protect me from you? Shelby wondered.

And so she had arrived at work Monday, eager for her life to be normal again. Maybe boring was a good thing, after all. The day flew by and when Shelby was preparing to head home for a quick supper before the regular monthly school board meeting, Catherine stopped her. "Are you sure you are okay to cover the meeting tonight? You look shot. I could cover it myself if you need to rest," she offered.

"I'll be fine," Shelby said flashing a perky smile and straightening her spine. "I want to see this story through. I'll grab a bite and freshen up and I'll be good as new," she promised.

Catherine was skeptical, but accepted Shelby's assurances. "See you in the morning, then." Shelby hurried away to get ready for the meeting.

Riley claimed a seat near the back of the room and now he surveyed the crowd that gathered for the school board meeting. He hadn't been reassured when the Brookings police had declared Shelby's accident just that, an accident. He and Andrew had told the Miller's Bend police about the last note that Shelby received while she was in Brookings. Even after they passed that information on to the Brookings investigators, they found no evidence that the vehicle was tampered with and no witnesses had come forth to say they had seen anything at the time of the accident. Oddly, the surveillance cameras in the area had no recordings for the time when the accident occurred. Riley didn't like the coincidence and vowed to keep an eye on Shelby until the Miller's Bend police could figure out whether there was a legitimate threat against her.

It had been several weeks since Shelby's last story about the athletic complex went to print and word spread throughout the county and the school district. It appeared that Steven wasn't the only person who had questions about the proposed complex. The room was packed with what Riley estimated to be upwards of 150 people, and more were still arriving.

Shelby had filled a seat in the second row with her bag and black wool coat. She, however, was standing near the front of the room involved in what looked to be an extremely intense conversation with one of the members of the school board. And she looked to be all business. She wore a gray suit with a silky-looking sapphire blouse that she had buttoned up to her chin. She even wore glasses. *To make herself look older? Wiser? More mature?* Riley smiled to himself, thinking that maybe he should get a pair of glasses, if that was the case.

The crowd of citizens continued to pack into the school board meeting room and into the school's central offices. It was becoming evident that the meeting would need to be in a different location. Mr. Jones was clearly growing aggravated as he made the announcement that the meeting would be moved to the school's theater, where he hoped there would be adequate seating for the audience. The use of the term "audience" had Riley envisioning a circus. As he registered the current of energy coursing through the crowd, he hoped the night didn't turn into a circus.

Well, there's the master of ceremonies, clowns, and people trying to sell us something. Maybe it is a circus, after all, he thought. The crowd murmured and groaned as people picked up their coats and began migrating to the theater.

Riley filed down the isle of the theater with the others who began filling seats from the back, except for few, like Shelby, who bolted toward the front hoping to get seats near the action. Riley paused near a row of seats that had some openings. Then he moved forward again, sidestepped into the row where Shelby had transferred her bag and coat and took the seat next to hers. A grin touched his lips as he wondered what her reaction would be. He scanned the seats behind him, which were rapidly filling; then he scanned the stage where the school custodian dashed about setting up tables and chairs for the board members. The IT man was getting the speaker system up and running, while Mr. Jones glared alternately at the two men, as though they had caused all of his problems.

Finally, Riley noticed Mr. Jones' gaze shift from the custodian to something beyond and followed the line of sight. Shelby. Nearly hidden on the far left of the stage, back in among the black theatrical curtains, Shelby had her back to the stage; her head bowed over her notebook, and was writing furiously. *Who is she talking with?* Riley wondered as he shifted his attention back to Jones. The man's face had flushed, eyebrows dipped low and deep scowl transformed his face in a mask of anger. He moved swiftly across the stage toward Shelby and her shadowy source.

Instinctively Riley rose from his seat simultaneously letting out a piercing whistle. The cacophony stilled, as did Jones. Riley felt the eyes on him and knew nearly 200 people were watching, but his focus was ahead on the man who towered at center stage frozen in midstride. "Hey, Jones!" he yelled. "You gonna get this show on the road sometime today?" So much for leaving youthful mischief behind.

Jones pivoted to face the members of the crowd, and Riley in particular. "Why, Mr. Wheeler," Jones addressed only Riley. "You know this is a serious meeting for serious minded folks. Why don't you ..." his voice trailed away as his beady eyes began to dart from face to face in the audience. He had their full attention as they hung on his words and took in his appearance – the aggressive stance, the agitation, the annoyance. Then as Riley and the rest watched, Jones morphed into the calm, commanding community leader they all had believed him to be.

Riley grinned widely at the discomfort Jones showed as the realization that he may have damaged his own image dawned on him. Riley split his attention between distracting Jones from interfering in Shelby's interview, and watching her make her escape from the darkened edges of the stage. Riley hadn't been able to discern to whom Shelby had been speaking – wasn't even sure whether it was it was a man or woman. Jones' gleaming eyes were back on Riley now, "As I was saying," the superintendent continued in an unnaturally sweet voice, "Why don't you join us on stage? You can be the first concerned citizen to address the board with your opinion and your concerns."

"Well, Mr. Jones," Riley replied in the most serene voice he could muster, "I just might take you up on that offer." Riley rotated to face the audience for a few seconds, spotted Shelby slipping in the main entrance and moving toward her seat. He swiveled back to face Jones once again and cleared his throat. "But I do believe that Robert's Rules of Order would have you call your meeting to order and perform your regular business prior to inviting public input." Riley paused, noting the rich red coloring in Jones skin as the man glared menacingly at Riley. "Wouldn't you agree, Mr. Jones?"

Riley stepped into the isle to let Shelby move into the row and take her seat. Then he moved in and sat next to her, all the while keeping his focus on Jones. The assembly seemed to hold its collective breath until Mr. Jones moved to his seat at the table and addressed the chairman of the board, "Let's get started," he growled.

"Where did you learn that?" she whispered fiercely.

"Learn what? How to tick off school officials? I think it was second grade," he quipped, accentuating the statement with the devilish smile of his.

"Actually, I meant the parliamentary procedure stuff," she hissed.

"Four-H. President of my club three years," he replied with his face too near hers, his eyes mesmerizing. "You should have seen me back then, you'd have loved me." She flushed and he turned his attention to the stage.

Shelby settled more deeply into her seat with her focus seemingly glued on the men and women on stage. Riley watched her out of the corner of his eye. Tension radiated from her slight frame, her shoulders squared, her pen at the ready, her lips pressed in a tight line, her eyes narrowed as she leaned forward in her seat intent on the proceedings of the school board. Riley leaned closer to Shelby, tipped his head, placing his lips near her perfectly formed ear, and as her hair tickled his cheek, he whispered lightly, "You're welcome." She shivered slightly. Riley shifted back into his seat, with his eyes on the stage, a smile on his lips and hope in his heart.

Two tortuous hours later the meeting was adjourned and the crowd was sent home. It had been a long meeting, and an extremely emotional one. Shelby hadn't realized that people of the community could be so attached to the old football field, but some of them certainly were. Riley left his seat without a word to Shelby as soon as the crowd began to disband, and the act left her feeling lonely. He could have at least said, "See ya". She would have to wait until later to think about Riley. Later there would be time to wonder why he had heckled Mr. Jones before the meeting even began.

CHAPTER TWENTY-FOUR

Shelby's mind was already moving into the story writing process as she packed her notebook, gold pen and eye glasses into her bag. They slid in beside the documents she'd received from an unexpected confidential source prior to the meeting and had discretely tucked into her bag. She was confident this story was going to turn out to be the stuff small town scandals are made of, but she would have to share this new information with the police.

The lead for tomorrow's story would be Steven Miller's statements, which were supported by several other citizens who also addressed the board. During the first meeting Miller had been the only person to speak out – to question the motives of the board.

Tonight's meeting showed Miller to be a much more competent speaker. He was also better prepared. He included some very interesting documentation indicating the school administration may have intentionally deferred maintenance on some issues with the old football field. Three different speakers shared first-hand knowledge that things had been "let go" to the point of being too costly to repair. This time additional questions were raised by prominent citizens as well as common folk. Shelby realized that she'd been lucky to have Riley beside her during the meeting, letting her know the names of speakers from the audience.

Never mind that it gave her little shivers and made her heart race each and every time he leaned close to whisper a name or other identifying information to her as she hurried to take notes on the comments they made.

Other than the board members and school personnel, Shelby was the last to leave the theater and file through the exit doors of the school building. The winter wind buffeted her, swirling loose tendrils of hair into her face. Icy snow stung her skin causing her to pull her coat up tighter. As she stepped off the curb, moving steadily toward her new used vehicle – a Dodge Charger – she felt inside her coat pockets for the keys and came up with nothing. She patted her pants pockets, feeling for the keys, and then remembered that she had worn a suit without pockets. She pulled her bag from her shoulder and rummaged through it as she slowed her steps, still heading for her car in the dimly lighted parking lot.

Riley had slipped from the theater as quickly as he could when the meeting adjourned. He'd started the engine in his pickup, cued his favorite playlist and waited for Shelby to emerge from the building. Now he watched as she came through the door trailing several minutes behind what had to be the last of the crowd from the meeting. Riley hadn't seen any of the board members or Mr. Jones exit the building. He was sure they were holding another "unofficial" strategy session.

Confident that she wanted to maintain her illusion of independence, and aware of the possibility that Shelby might not have appreciated him claiming the seat right next to her for the meeting, Riley had decided to slip quickly outside and wait for her there. He knew she wanted to emit the image of a professional, and he doubted that having her fiancé clinging to her would be in keeping with that image. So he decided to give her room – as much as he dared considering the threats she had been receiving. He would just wait until she was in her car, and then follow her back to Mrs. Holmes' place.

Shelby's steps slowed as she began to search through her pockets, and then began patting herself here and there. Riley smiled as her expression changed from focus and determination to confusion and frustration. She pulled her bag from her shoulder and hugged it in front of herself with her left arm as she began rifling through the contents. She continued walking in the general direction of her car with her head down, her attention riveted on an apparent search for something. *She's lost her keys.* Then Riley noticed movement at the edge of the shadows west of the main entrance. His curiosity piqued as he realized a person had been obscured in the darkness. *Who? Why?*

Suddenly Riley could envision what was about to happen. The man – Riley was certain that it was a man – moved stealthily toward the unsuspecting woman with her nose in her bag. Walking in high heeled shoes across the snow-packed pavement, she wouldn't have chance to outrun or fight off the mystery man who was gaining on her. Riley laid on the horn for seconds before he leaped from the truck yelling, "Here! Over here!"

Shelby heard the blare of a car horn in the parking lot and jerked her head up from her bag. Her spiky little shoe let her left foot slip wildly on the smooth surface and as she fought to keep her balance, her mind processed the fact that Riley was bolting toward her and yelling – he was frantic. The heels of both Shelby's shoes scraped through the packed snow grabbing traction beneath and she steadied momentarily. Confusion coursed through Shelby as she looked left, then right, pivoting a quarter turn to glance behind her, she spotted a shadowy figure a second before the hard mass of a man slammed into her.

Shelby's scream sliced through the night air as the breath swooshed from her lungs. The momentum from the hit had the two bodies sliding across the traffic lane on the snowy surface. Her skull hammered against the frozen ground as Shelby's slight five foot, 120 pound frame acted as a toboggan for the attacker who was easily double her weight. Something crashed into her left jawbone then pressed painfully against her throat. Terror flashed through Shelby as she fought to breathe. Fear that she could die was quickly replaced by determination not to let that happen. Desperation had her clawing the man's face – digging for his eyes – scratching any flesh she could contact.

Suddenly he was gone. She could breathe again. Shelby lay in the snow, the muscles in her torso convulsed as her traumatized lungs worked to gain oxygen again. She wheezed slightly as the air passed through her bruised throat. Her pulse pounded in her head and every single body part she could feel ached. Then the shivers started racking her body.

Riley had been within yards of Shelby when the assailant had launched himself at her. Riley felt a peculiar, gut-wrenching dread as he witnessed the hit followed by Shelby's petite body slamming onto the snow-packed pavement. Then there was the crushing mass of the attacker smashing onto her. *God protect her. Help me help her.* Riley's silent plea went up instantly. Two more strides and Riley hurled himself at the shoulders of the assailant. The force of the collision bulldozed the man clear of Shelby's beaten body. The attacker's head cracked against the frozen ground with a sickening thump. His body went limp.

"Shel?" Riley called out as he scrambled to her side. "Shelby!" He slid to a stop on his knees beside her still body. "Dear God, please..." He was hitting the last digit in 911 as Riley realized people had gathered behind him.

"Ambulance is on the way. So is the police chief," an authoritative voice boomed. "Can you explain what happened here?"

Riley felt the urge to face down the authority figure, and the accusation in Jones' voice. Then the senseless feeling was lost in a sea of emotions directed only at Shelby. He focused on her face – eyes closed, brows drawn down, bruises developing on her face and neck. Her tender pink lips moved slightly and his heart clenched. "Shelby, please, please. Be okay," he whispered only for her hearing. "Help is on the way, honey. Just hold on!"

Eyelashes fluttered slightly before Shelby licked her lips lightly. "Thanks," she scarcely could get the word out. Shelby winced. Riley was rocked with rage – slammed his fist into his thigh. "Oh, Shelby, I'm so sorry I didn't get to him in time," he rasped out.

"'s okay," she responded with a slight smile. A new set of shivers shook her body and Riley stripped his coat off, gently placing it over Shelby.

"Mr. Jones called for the ambulance, it'll be here in a minute," he assured her quietly. Blue eyes flew open wide; a trembling mouth formed the word "no" but without sound. She moved as though trying to look toward the school building.

Riley placed a hand gently to her shoulder. The other massaged her cheek as his features drew into a scowl. "Stay still, you need to go to the hospital," he said softly. "They're close. Hear the sirens?"

Shelby's head jerked toward Riley. Her eyes drifted closed then snapped open again. "M ... bag ... important," she pushed the sound past her lips. "Please?"

Riley glanced around not understanding her concern about the bag? "Don't worry about it. Just stay still until the paramedics get here," he pleaded. His hand continued to stroke her cheek, smoothing her hair back, calming both of them.

Ice cold fingers caught his just as her gaze locked on Riley's. "'s important," she whispered, "Jones wants..." At the mention of the man's name, Riley swung his head toward the group – the school board and Mr. Jones. They had migrated as a unit from the sidewalk, to near where the assault had occurred. They stood, flanking Jones. And behind them lay Shelby's bag. Their faces and stances mirrored varying degrees of concern and worry. Some even looked agitated, fearful or something else, something nastier. And Jones emitted undeniable hostility.

What am I missing? Riley wondered. *This is all wrong. Why would someone attack Shelby? What's with the bag? What's with the school board?*

Then police chief was beside Shelby, kneeling near her, checking her pulse, talking into the radio mic Velcroed to his shoulder. Finally he spoke to the still woman. "Shelby?" he queried, "Can you hear me, Shelby?" Riley's hands hadn't left their tasks of gently holding her still and soothing her. The actions were keeping him calm as his mind tried to piece together the bigger picture, while subconsciously sending prayers heavenward.

EMTs appeared beside each of the apparent victims, and after a brief radio message, the chief shifted his focus to Riley. "Tell me what happened." It was a command, not a question and Riley felt the old familiar defensiveness rise within himself. He breathed in deeply, rotated, taking in the scene around him. Noting that Jones was near Shelby's bag and it's scattered belongings he suddenly realized what she had been trying to tell him.

Her notes from the meeting are in the bag, as well as her notes from the covert conversation with the secret source in the shadows before the meeting. Did she have something more in her bag? Did she have the evidence she had been searching for? The evidence someone was willing to hurt, or kill, to keep hidden?

"I will gladly tell you everything I know, but, please let me go grab Shelby's bag and her belongings like she asked me to," Riley responded, looking the chief square in the eye. The man assessed Riley, and then he nodded as the two moved in tandem toward the cluster of board members. Jones had stopped and was reaching for Shelby's bag that lay in the snow.

"Hold it!" the chief commanded sternly. Jones straightened, clenching the bag in his hands. He looked furtively around, glancing to each board member as they shifted away from him, widening the arc encircling the superintendent. The chief held his hand toward the bag, "Thank you, Art. But when I say 'hold it' I don't mean 'keep on doing what you're doing,'" he said as he seized the bag from Jones. Keeping his focus on Jones, the officer continued, "Mr. Wheeler, you may, as per the victim's request, collect her possessions and take them with you to the hospital where I am certain I will find you in a few minutes."

Riley accepted the bag noting the red stain of blood on his right hand. Whose blood? He hadn't noticed that any of them was bleeding. Looking back to the scene where Shelby's inert form was being hoisted into the ambulance, Riley nodded. His eyes returned to the chief's, "Yes sir. Thank you," Riley said as he swallowed hard. "That's where I'll be." Additional officers and a second ambulance had arrived. The attacker sat in the open back doorway of the unit with EMTs evaluating him. The chief directed an officer to take the witnesses inside and keep them from talking with each other until he joined them.

"Riley," the man cleared his throat. "I'm going to need a really clear account of what happened here when I talk to you." He glanced meaningfully at the school building doors as they closed behind the pack of officials that had just passed through. "I have a feeling that I'll get mixed reports." He looked emphatically at Shelby's bag. "Keep that with you. Don't leave it in your truck. I'm going to want to go through it when I catch up with you."

Riley nodded, "Thanks. I'll be at the hospital." He moved toward his truck which was still running.

CHAPTER TWENTY-FIVE

When Riley entered the hospital, carrying Shelby's bag tucked under his arm like a football, he drew the attention of the women at the nurses' station. "Why Riley Wheeler, what on earth are you doing here? Are you hurt?" one of his mother's friends, LeAnn, asked. Unsure of his voice, Riley simply shook his head. LeAnn spotted the bundle nestled against his side and added, "If you've brought me a present, you can set it there," she indicated the desktop, "we're really busy right now. Two traumas just came in." She scurried past him in continuation of the task she'd been performing.

"I know. How's Shelby?" he asked in a voice that trembled slightly. LeAnn paused taking in Riley's appearance – his skin was pale, his eyes pained, distress radiated from his body, his clothing had wet spots, mud and grime, and on his hand she noted the dried blood.

"Maria!" LeAnn called out. "Maria. Take these supplies to room one. I'm taking Mr. Wheeler to room three. He needs medical evaluation," she directed as she handed the supplies to the passing Maria, and guided Riley down the hall toward an empty room.

"How's Shelby?" Riley repeated, as he allowed LeAnn to lead him. At the entrance to the room, he balked. "I need to see Shelby."

She pressed him into the room, "No. You need to be evaluated," she insisted. Riley spun away from LeAnn's hold, turning to leave the room, only to be met by a third nurse who temporarily blocked the doorway. "Oh, no you don't, Riley. You get right back over here," LeAnn said as she steered him again toward an exam table. "Sit."

He sat. He sat clutching Shelby's bag in his lap, wondering why LeAnn wouldn't tell him Shelby's condition. *It's bad. She must be in really bad shape.* Riley began to register the sounds in the hallway and in nearby rooms. His gaze locked on her face, "LeAnn. Talk to me, please," he begged. "How's Shelby?"

LeAnn paused and absorbed Riley's distraught expression. She sighed. "I cannot tell you anything about other patients," she finally commented. "You should know that. I can only reveal details to family."

"I am family!" he roared.

"No."

"We're engaged. She's my fiancée."

"Oh, Riley! Your Momma must be so happy," she beamed for a second before her expression changed again. "But I still can't tell you anything."

"I love her with everything I am," he wailed. "I can't lose her!"

Calmly rubbing Riley's shoulder, LeAnn offered, "I'm really sorry. I cannot tell you anything. But, if I could trust you to behave for Maria to evaluate you, I could go help in another room, where my years of experience might be needed." She paused. "Would you do that for me? For Shelby? Sit here and behave until I can get back to you?"

He nodded. "I'll stay here," he said with resignation. "Tell her I ... tell her I'm praying for her," he added as LeAnn headed for the other room.

Maria appeared inside of a minute, looking a bit apprehensive. "LeAnn says to tell you that I can't tell you anything," she warned. He nodded again. Maria began working to evaluate Riley's condition, recording notes in his chart, looking for wounds or serious injury. She announced that he was fine and after letting him clean up, moved him to another room. Not the waiting room, which he had expected, but a private room with a table and chairs, and a police officer.

Riley indicated a plastic chair nestled against the edge of the table, "May I?" he inquired of Officer Pendleton.

"By all means, have a seat. The chief will be here shortly. He asked me to keep you company until he arrives," came the easy response. The men assessed each other coolly for a few moments. Finally, the door opened again and both zeroed in on the form of Chief Jeff Schuster as he filled the doorway. His expression was completely neutral, his face giving no hint as to the status of the victims, or information retrieved during the interviews of the witnesses.

"Mr. Wheeler," he said by way of greeting. He nodded toward the younger officer, "Josh. I need you to go wait for the blood tests," he extended his hand toward the door. "Report back immediately when you have the results."

"Yes, sir," he replied, rising from his seat at the table. Pendleton made eye contact with Riley, "I'll see if I can get an update on the young lady's condition, too."

Riley had risen with Pendleton. Now Riley and Chief Schuster faced each other squarely. "Chief," Riley began, "Can you tell me anything?"

"Riley, I've known you for about twenty years and I don't believe you have ever once called me 'Chief'." The town's senior police officer stepped closer to Riley. He thumped the younger man on the shoulder, and then slid his hand up to squeeze the back of his neck, as he had done when Riley was in trouble when he was elementary school aged. "Let's have a seat and go over some things."

Jeff Schuster had been a fixture in Riley's life since Riley and Tyler, Jeff's son, had each tried to pummel the other in first grade. Their third buddy, Matt, had joined them in middle school, when his family moved to town. The trio became "the posse" before they graduated from high school five years later. Jeff, now in his 50s, had worked his way up through the department to the rank of police chief.

Privately he and Riley's father had watched the boys live, fight, learn the lessons of teenage love, and then sent them off to vocational school. When they had finished their schooling the men welcomed them home with pride.

Professionally Jeff had seen the boys through varied traumas, confrontations and dilemmas. He had never been in the position of having to charge any of the three with a crime, although they were close on a couple of occasions. He felt honored that he'd had a role in forming them into the men the three friends were today.

Riley couldn't recall ever being as glad to see someone in an emergency as he had been to see Tyler's father at Shelby's side on the icy pavement hours before. Riley, distraught over

Shelby's condition, was furious at the attacker and struggling to remain calm. All the while he'd been trying to decipher exactly what had happened - why Shelby had been targeted.

Jeff guided Riley back to a chair and produced a soda, "Have a drink. Get some sugar into your system." With Shelby's bag cradled in his lap, Riley gulped the cold beverage. After a minute, he raised his gaze to the older man. The father-figure was gone and the police chief had resurfaced, "Now. Explain your ... relationship ... to the victim, Shelby Sweetin."

Riley paused. He took another swig from the bottle and regarded the label with an intensity that was completely unreasonable. *Relationship?* The chief cleared his throat, "Riley, that's the easy question. How do you know Shelby? It's going to get more difficult from here."

"She's the part of me that was missing all those years. She completes me. She makes me whole. She keeps me sane while she makes me crazy. And she will be my wife," Riley spoke quietly, almost reverently.

"How did you meet?"

"You've got to be kidding. She could be dying in there and you want to know how we met!"

"She's not dying," the chief confided. "Until I get permission from her parents, I can't tell you anything."

Riley growled in frustration.

"That's how it is," the chief glared at Riley. "Now, how did you meet?"

Riley clutched Shelby's bag to his chest as he began telling their story to the chief. Emotions and desperation tore at Riley and he was afraid he would break down. He remembered the detachment Shelby had shown when recounting the experience of the bank robbery. Taking a cue from her, he locked his emotions away. Setting the bag roughly on the table he turned away. When he faced the chief again he was granite-hard and emotionally cold.

With detachment Riley told the tale of their stormy friendship, Mrs. Holmes certainty that they belonged together, his jealousy when she was meeting with Andrew, her tenaciousness about the school board story. His control was slipping by the time he talked his way through the threats against her and the accident in Brookings. Andrew and his friend, Mason Alexander, arrived just as Riley was relating his certainty that someone had been trying to kill her when her Jeep had gone off the overpass.

The chief rose and extended a hand to welcome the new arrivals, "Andrew. Mason. What brings you in, Mason?"

"Oh, I was just hanging out with Andrew, when he got the call that his little brother was being interrogated without representation, so I thought I'd tag along," the young lawyer explained with a smile.

"We are just chatting while we wait to see how Miss Sweetin is doing," the chief replied mildly.

"I'm confident you know how she's doing, Chief," Andrew said. "How are you holding up?" he directed the question to his younger brother who looked like … well, he looked pretty rough. "Did you get to the part where we've all been taking turns guarding Shelby until the police can figure out who's trying to hurt her?" He glared at the chief.

"You all?"

"Riley, Matt, Tyler and myself."

"Ty's in on this?" the chief sounded mystified.

"Yes."

Pendleton slipped back into the room and handed a folder to the chief. "She woke up and asked for Mr. Wheeler," he said, but was already signaling for Riley to stay put. Disregarding the signal, Riley charged for the door as the need to see Shelby caught fire and burned through him. A desperate growl emanated from his throat when Andrew and Mason blocked his way. "She gave verbal permission for Riley to have full access to her and her medical information, but the doctor is drugging her so she'll sleep," Pendleton explained. Looking to Riley again, he added, "I'm sorry, but she's already out again."

Fury shot through Riley with profound sorrow in its wake. He'd missed his chance to talk to her, to tell her he loved her and he wouldn't leave her side. He turned on Chief Schuster, "What about the attacker?"

"You mean victim number two?" the chief volleyed.

"No. I mean the man who attacked Shelby tonight. He is no victim," Riley spat. "He hid in the shadows and slithered up behind her until he was close enough to attack her!"

"That so?"

"Yes, that's so! I saw the whole thing from my truck," Riley continued. "I sat by her in the meeting, then I left right away. I started the truck and sat there waiting for her so I could follow her to Mrs. Holmes' place to keep her safe from the guy who's been threatening her for weeks. You know – the one who tried to run her down in the street; the one who broke into her apartment; the one who has been stalking and threatening her. The one who almost killed her when she was in Brookings! The man who attacked her from out of the shadows tonight. The one who would have beaten her to death there on the ice in the parking lot of the school while no one did anything to stop him!"

The room reverberated with the energy of Riley's rage. Four men waited for his fury to spill over, but Riley managed to rein it in. He moved menacingly into the Chief's space with his face inches from the older man's. Pendleton started to move forward to aid his superior but Schuster waived him off. "That's your victim number two," Riley hissed. "If you believe he's a victim, then you're not the man I thought you were."

"Riley! That's enough!" Andrew stepped in. Lowering his voice, he repeated, "That's enough."

"I trust you got what you wanted here," the lawyer said calmly as he flanked Riley.

"I did," he replied to Mason. Turning to Riley, he added, "Sorry about the method, but I needed your account of tonight's incident and I needed to see the passion behind it."

Riley didn't respond.

"The reports from the school board members vary a great deal," he offered. "They heard Shelby scream and rushed outside. Some think they saw you attack both Shelby and the man; some think they saw you saving Shelby; some think they saw the man attack you and Shelby together."

"You thought I could have attacked them?" Riley asked incredulously. "You know me better than that!"

"Maybe she was dating him and you were jealous … could have happened that way," the chief said offhandedly, as though it were nothing. "At any rate your story pretty much matches the attacker's story."

Riley seethed. "You talked to him?"

"Well, yah," the chief smiled. "That's part of how we investigate."

"What did he say? Why has he been after her? Is he the embezzler or was he hired to do this?" Riley fired the questions. "How long will he rot in prison?"

"All your questions will be answered in time, Riley," the chief replied. "We haven't gotten to the bottom of this yet. But we do know that you are not the aggressor here, so you won't be charged with anything. You can go home, Riley."

"No I can't," Riley countered. "I'll be in her room keeping her safe and you will not stop me." He shot a scathing look at the chief and flung the door open.

"You have the attacker in custody, Chief?" Mason asked casually as he watched Riley's rapid progress toward the nurses' station with Andrew following his brother at a more leisurely pace. "We don't want anything to happen to him, do we?"

"We transferred him to the county jail. He's got an EMT with him for medical supervision. He should be fine there," Schuster said with a nod. "Pendleton, take Miss Sweetin's bag and belongings back to the office please. And don't let it out of your sight."

"What about those blood tests, Chief?" Mason asked with a deceptively casual attitude.

Schuster rocked back on his heels, assessing the man. "Are you representing someone?"

Mason nodded. "What about the blood and tissue?" he repeated.

"The tissue and blood under the victim's fingernails -"

"Shelby's nails," Mason corrected.

The chief glared at the young lawyer, "– definitely belonged to the assailant. Apparently, she got a few good swipes in before Riley got to him."

"What else?"

"There was blood on Riley's hand, but it turns out that it was Shelby's. Probably from when he was trying to help her, comfort her," the chief explained. "We couldn't detect any blood or tissue exchange between Riley and the assailant."

"So there's no chance you'll change your stance and charge Riley with anything?" Mason challenged.

"None that I can foresee," the chief responded. "The state's attorney will have a look at the evidence, but I don't know any reason he would interpret it differently."

CHAPTER TWENTY-SIX

Shelby moaned as her mind registered the misery that pulsed through her body. *What happened?* She raised a hand to her pounding head and pain shot through her shoulder and radiated down her back. She gasped at the suddenness and severity of the anguish that coursed through her body.

Big mistake! The gasp caused a spasm of agony through her torso. A hand was on her shoulder, another stroking her cheek again. *Again?* Then she heard the soft voice of her mother, "Hey, Sweetie," she murmured. "Just lie still, for a bit. The more you move around the more it's going to hurt." Shelby heard a sniffling sound followed by shuffled footsteps; another hand came to rest on her other shoulder. *Dad.* Shelby tried a smile and was glad it didn't cause any additional pain. *Thank you, God. I'm alive, and loved.*

She opened her eyes to find two of her most precious faces intently hovering before her. "Hi," she croaked quietly. "What happened?" she whispered, glancing from one to the other. They exchanged looks.

"We can talk about it later, Sweetie," Mom said in a placating tone. "Now you need to drink lots of water and rest."

"And let the doctor know you're awake," Dad added. "Come on, Molly, let's go talk to the nurse and leave these two alone a minute."

Two? Shelby touched her mom's arm lightly and the movement shot renewed pain through her ribcage. Wincing again, Shelby focused on her mother's face. "Who's here?"

Then Riley's face appeared where her father's had been a moment before. "Hi, ya," he said with a small smile. Relief coursed through Shelby and a smile bloomed on her bruised face.

"Thank you," Shelby's voice squeaked as she started to speak, then her throat caught. It felt wonderful to see Riley before her; but he looked like ten miles of bad country road. She drank in the image of him with whiskers darkening his face, fatigue in his eyes, stress lines by those warm caramelly eyes and around his mouth, ruffled hair ... until the image began to shimmer and waver. She sniffled.

"Hey, hey. Come on ... don't cry now," he offered soothingly. Riley tenderly placed a light kiss on her cheek before pulling back to search her eyes. "Are you hurting? I can tell the nurse to hurry," concern etched his voice as he straightened again.

"No," the answer was soft, so soft. "I'm just glad to see you," Shelby smiled. Riley was consumed by emotions that he'd been holding at bay. *Thank you, God, for saving Shelby's life and starting her progress in healing.*

"What happened?" she asked searching his face when he didn't answer. "You were there ..." her voice cracked as images flashed in her mind: a frantic Riley barreling toward her, a shadow of a man behind her, and the explosion of pain.

The terror of the seconds the man was upon her returned. She jerked her face away from Riley's piercing gaze, causing pain to ricochet through her head and shoulders again.

Shelby's right cheek and left shoulder were the only places Riley had found that touching her hadn't made her wince when she was unconscious, and now his hands automatically migrated back to those safe zones. The backs of his fingers grazed her cheek gently. "It'll be okay, Shel," he crooned soothingly. "You're already healing. It'll be okay." He tenderly tipped her face back toward his. Placing a whisper light kiss on the cheek where his fingers had been he rose from the edge of the bed. "I better go. For now," he added softly.

Shelby's eyes followed Riley's form to the door which had burst open with the return of her parents and the arrival of Dr. Strapp and a nurse. The doctor systematically evaluated Shelby before grimly marking mysterious notations on her chart, reassuring Shelby and her parents that she was on the road to recovery and then retreating from the room.

"Mom," Shelby said weakly. "Tell me what happened."

"You're too tired to talk anymore right now," her mother hedged as she glanced to Shelby's father, Jack. Shelby turned her head to look at him.

"Dad?" she begged. "Please tell me what's going on."

Jack stood gazing out the window but seeing nothing. His shoulders shifted with a deep sigh and he rotated them slightly as though attempting to relieve stress or pain. He had raised four of his five children to adulthood without ever spending a night pacing and worrying in a hospital waiting room like he had Monday night. And all day Tuesday. He couldn't recall Wednesday – other than that it had been a mix of worrying, pacing, and praying. By that night he'd been exhausted enough to sleep lightly in the chair. The pacing resumed Thursday, until Shelby had awakened less than an hour ago.

He had never imagined the anguish that parents suffer at helplessly watching one of their children lay sleeping for more than 48 hours, while God works to heal their body. Waiting for them to awaken. Praying for their healing. Waiting to learn if their mind had been spared damage in the accident, or in this case in the attack.

"Dad," she repeated with more force. "We've never lied to each other. I can't believe you want to start now."

"Shelby, that's not fair!" her mother interjected. "Your father and I -"

"Fair? You want to talk about fair, Mom?" Shelby's face, moments ago pale from pain and stress, flushed with anger. "I was attacked, Mom! Attacked! And I just want to know what happened and nobody will tell me! What's fair about that?" she raged.

"Ladies," Jack intervened verbally, and physically, as he stepped beside Molly. He wrapped an arm around his wife of 36 years and squeezed her close. Molly dropped her head to Jack's shoulder. He kissed her blond head and pivoted toward a chair, where he gently guided her to a sitting position. Jack returned to Shelby's side almost before she realized how easily her father had defused the rising emotional storm. "Shelby, there are more important things right now than telling you what happened when you were ... attacked."

For the first time, Shelby realized that tears stood in her father's eyes. She'd been confused and frightened. She wanted to know why she'd been attacked. She had dozens of questions – questions her parents probably didn't even have answers to.

But in her need for answers, Shelby failed to realize the impact her condition was waging on her parents. "I'm sorry, Daddy … Mom," she squeaked and sniffled. "I just …" *I just what?* "I'm just glad I have you two and that you love me enough to stay with me for …," her voice trailed away. Jack watched as Shelby's focus went to the dry erase board on the wall. On it was posted a colorful message: Today is Thursday. Your doctor is Dr. Strapp. The nurse on duty is Marie. Her brows drew down and together, her mouth formed a frown.

"Thursday? It's Thursday?" she asked incredulously. "That can't be right! The meeting was Monday. This is Tuesday," she rambled, grabbing at the blankets to pull them back, "I've got to write my story." Jack touched her arm, preventing any more movement before Shelby's mind registered the renewed pain that came when she reached for the blankets.

"It is Thursday. Stay in bed, you are not writing any stories today," he said calmly, while tucking the covers snugly but gently back around Shelby. "Your mother and I love you. We'll be here as long as you need us, and we can talk when you've rested."

The next time she awoke, Shelby looked around until her gaze landed on Riley who slept in the chair by the window. She had been having dreams – wild, varied dreams. Riley was in each of them, either leading her through a maze, miraculously stopping her Jeep from careening over the bridge railing, or pulling the man who had brutally attacked her away. In one dream, they were standing at the altar of her hometown church – she in a flowing white dress and he in a snappy tuxedo. In the mystical way one's mind maneuvers through a dream, suddenly they were old and gray, surrounded by grandchildren the next moment.

She slowly and carefully turned onto her side, so she could watch the man she loved. He had apparently gone home and gotten some rest. His clothing was no longer rumpled; his face clean shaven so his dimples showed again, his hair was once again in place. With his arms folded across his chest, he breathed slowly as he slept. How long had he stayed at the hospital? Maybe he and her parents had traded off staying in the room with her – watching over her, praying for her recovery, showering her with their love. Three of the people she loved most in the world, together …

"Oh, no!" she gasped as she realized that her fiancé and her parents had probably spent a whole lot of time getting to know each other without her to introduce them or guide the conversations. Carefully she laid her hands in front of her face as she imagined the way things had gone.

She sensed that Riley was near her bed a second before he gingerly tugged her hands away from her face. Concern etched his expression, "Are you in pain?" he asked when his eyes met hers. "I'll call the nurse …"

"No. Riley…" she began but then stalled. What did she need to say? "Thank you," she croaked. "You saved my life."

He shook his head. "No, you saved yourself, I just helped a little," he said. "Not enough, though." His brows were drawn down into a scowl, "… I almost didn't get to you in time." With jerky movements, she reached up to stroke the cheek of the man who she realized now she would love until her dying day.

"No, Riley," she whispered. "It worked out fine. I'll be alright. We'll be together and we will be just fine."

"You can't imagine what we've been through, Shelby. I felt so helpless, just watching you for days. I couldn't do anything to help you. Are you sure you don't need anything, right now?"

"Just you," she replied with a weak smile. "Help me sit up?"

When he had arranged her pillows and helped Shelby get positioned comfortably, she looked at her hands folded in her lap. The engagement ring glistened cheerily. "What about my parents?"

"They're at your apartment for a while," he responded. "You want me to call them?"

"No. I meant what did you and they talked about all these days?" she clarified as she raised her left hand, tipping it so the light caught in the diamond.

"Ah," Riley responded. "Well, I had to explain my presence. And the ring. But after that, we've been getting along pretty well," he said with a sincere smile. "You dad's quite a character. I can't imagine raising a whole herd of girls," he said shaking his head as he smiled. He picked up Shelby's small hands in his own and tenderly kissed the hand that bore his ring. "I wouldn't mind trying it with you though," he added.

Overwhelmed with emotions, Shelby pulled her hands free from Riley's and slid them to his sides, then on around to his back. He let her tug him forward, leaning into her embrace until their lips were inches apart. "I was so scared that I'd lose you, Shelby," he confided quietly.

"Never. You'll never lose me, Riley," she assured him. "As long as I can draw a breath, I'll be yours."

The kiss that followed was sweet and tender, but also promised a lifetime of commitment and love. Riley held her close to his heart and she clung to him for a long time as the two reveled in the simple pleasure of knowing they would be together. God had his plan for them and they were ready to listen and follow that plan.

A knock at the door broke the serenity of the moment. Police Chief Jeff Schuster let himself into the room, saying that he needed to get her official statement. Riley excused himself, kissed Shelby softly on the cheek and said he'd be back after running some errands. After Shelby told her story of the attack to the police chief, she learned that he was a man who had been like a second father to Riley through the years. The man clearly loved Riley and had been distraught at the possibility that he had needed to consider Riley as a suspect for even a few hours at the time of the attack.

After recording her statement, Jeff Schuster hugged Shelby and congratulated her on the engagement. "He's bound to be a handful," the man said, "but I'm sure that'll just help keep things fresh for you. And you'll never have to doubt his commitment – I saw the depth of emotion he has for you that night."

"I know now," she said. "It took me a while to trust him – to trust my feelings. But I know we won't fail each other. Love never fails."

The chief also explained to Shelby that her assailant had confessed to stalking her, to delivering the threats and breaking into her apartment. He had been the almost-hit-and-run driver and tampered with her Jeep, causing the accident in Brookings.

"But why?" she asked. "Why would anyone involved in the embezzlement case want to add attempted murder to the list of offenses?" she wondered aloud.

"The embezzlement?" Schuster echoed. "He wasn't connected to that at all. This was about the robbery you witnessed a couple years ago. Your testimony put his half-brother in prison for life."

Shelby paled. *The robbery! Of course!* "Ashley and Allison?" she asked as panic rose within her. "Was he the man who attacked Allison, too?"

Schuster nodded. "He was going to get you all," he confirmed. "Apparently he thought Allison was dead after he attacked her. Then you showed up in Brookings alone and it was easier for him to get to you there than it had been here where you were here – spending so much time with Riley and the boys."

"Did anyone contact Ashley? Is she safe?" Shelby's concern for her friends overwhelmed her. She moved as if to get out of the bed but sudden pain made her gasp and fall back to the pillows.

"Stay put. With the help of your family and Riley, we figured out who to check on and took care of it. Allison hadn't had any problems since your visit, and apparently, the attacker hadn't set his sights on Ashley yet. You were his top priority."

"Now what happens?" she asked nervously. She remembered the months of testimony and preparation for the robbery trial and had no desire to go through that again. "I suppose we will all have to testify ..." she said with a grimace.

"Not this time," the chief said despondently. Shelby looked at the man curiously. He suddenly looked much older than he did when he was talking about the young couple and their future together. He shook his head and answered her unspoken question, "The poor soul. We transferred him to Brookings for holding until his hearing because it's a larger facility with more staff and more resources. Somehow he managed to kill himself while being held there." The chief paused before looking Shelby in the eye, "Honestly, I appreciate not having to go through everything involved in prosecuting and you'll never have to worry about him being paroled, but it's sad that he saw suicide as his only option."

"His poor family. They must be devastated," she said. "How will they cope with one son in prison and one dead?"

"It was just the two of them," Schuster explained. "Apparently it had been just the two of them against the world for several years."

"We should pray for them both. Can you ask the pastor to include them in the prayer requests Sunday?" she said quietly. "I don't think I'll be out of here by then."

CHAPTER TWENTY-SEVEN

Riley's mind wandered as he stood gazing out the window of the hotel room overlooking the sprawling landscape of Rapid City in Western South Dakota. His ears picked up the strains of the country music video paying on TV as Brad Paisley crooned about the poor men who were "waitin' on a woman" and he smiled to himself. "Are you about ready, honey?" he asked toward the closed bathroom door.

"Almost," came the muffled reply. It was followed by the sound of something bouncing off the counter and clattering to the floor.

"You know our dinner reservation is in fifteen minutes," he reminded gently, as he glanced at the clock on the nightstand. "Should I call and cancel?" he teased, not expecting a response.

Again looking out over the city, Riley remembered the days and weeks that followed the attack on Shelby. Once released from the hospital, she had gone back to the apartment where her parents planned to stay with her. He snorted as he recalled Shelby's response to that plan. "I'm a big girl and this is my place," she said hugging her dad and mom in turn. "I appreciate the offer, but I think I'd rest better if I'm alone. Have you looked into the Super 8?"

Mrs. Holmes, who had been busy making tea and arranging sugar cookies to be served in Shelby's apartment when they arrived, suggested a possible solution. "Your folks can stay in the spare room upstairs, dear," she offered. "That way they are close by so they won't worry, but will still be … out of your hair," she concluded as she looked between Shelby and Riley.

Shelby blushed. Riley watched as the rich pink blossomed beneath the bruises on her face and neck. He loved her. He loved that blush. But, oh how he hated those bruises. Just looking at them brought back the fear that had clutched at his heart during the attack, and dominated him as he waited helplessly on the frozen parking lot pavement for help to arrive.

Once she was back in her apartment, Shelby recovered amazingly quickly. Her parents returned to their home a few days after she was released from the hospital, saying they were confident she was in good hands. With the help of their friends and Riley's family, the couple planned and pulled off a beautifully simple wedding near the end of January. The ceremony wasn't fancy. It wasn't flamboyant. It wasn't dramatic. They had endured enough drama.

He remembered now how people had expressed concern that a wedding couldn't be orchestrated so quickly and Riley responded that when Shelby Sweetin sets her mind to plan an event, it will happen. He questioned her privately though, "Are you sure you don't want a big impressive wedding? What about the fairy tale wedding that all little girls dream of?"

She had smiled as though she knew a very private secret before she replied. "Riley James Wheeler. I'm shocked that you don't know me better than that," she said in mock dismay. "It's not the wedding ceremony that's important. It's the marriage that's important." She kissed him before adding, "God didn't go to all this trouble to bring us together for a one-day event. He wants us to be happy together for a lifetime. And that's what I want, too."

The wedding was small and dignified. Surrounded by family and friends, Shelby and Riley had reverently taken their vows before God to love, honor and cherish each other all the days that they both shall live. They stood there at the altar with the love of God, the love they felt for each other and the love of their families washing around them. Riley remembered the feeling being so strong and absolutely right. He had struggled to try to put words to the feeling in the days following the ceremony, but as yet he couldn't manage to find them. He was just enjoying living in those feelings.

The eight hour drive across the state had been a pleasant one as the couple left for a brief honeymoon the following day. Shelby received a phone call shortly before noon while they were nearing the state capitol, Pierre. She glanced at Riley with a question in her eye.

"You may as well answer it," he replied with a grin. "Otherwise you'll just have to call them back."

When she had finished the conversation on the phone, she turned to Riley and announced, "That was Chief Schuster. He wanted to let us know that charges have been filed in the embezzlement case at the school."

"Against ...?" he prodded as he glanced toward Shelby and back to the road.

"You won't believe it," she predicted. He looked again at the crazy, stubborn woman he loved.

"Try me."

"Okay. It was the secretaries," she replied with a shake of her head. "Their story is that they set out to prove that the men are overpaid and don't really know what's going on. So they started syphoning money to see how long it would be before Jones and the others would notice."

"You're kidding."

"Apparently, Jones caught on that money was disappearing. Eventually. But he couldn't figure out how or where it was going, so he stayed quiet," she explained. "I've no idea how they passed the annual audits."

"What did they do with the money?"

"Put it aside. Didn't spend a dime, he said," she repeated. "Chief said they were so relieved when the police caught them. Once they had started taking the money, they weren't sure how to return it without raising red flags. The police have it all for now."

"The school district will get it back?"

"Sooner or later, I guess," she answered before slipping into silence.

After they had eaten in Pierre and were back on the road headed west, Shelby asked, "What do you think they feel like?" She pointed toward a group of pronghorn antelope sprinting toward a distant butte.

"Firm and hairy," Riley replied seconds before Shelby swatted his shoulder lightly.

"That's not what I meant," she huffed. "My heart feels like …."

Riley shifted so he could swing his right arm over her head and rest it on her shoulders. He pulled her closer and dropped a light kiss to her forehead. "Feels like what?" he asked cautiously. When she didn't answer, he asked, "Is something wrong?"

"Wrong? No!" She was looking up at him with her expression full of love and trust.

"What is it?"

"Well … When we first knew each other – before we were dating – Dad had a talk with me. He told me I had locked myself up, like a horse kept in a stall, so I would feel safe," she spoke slowly while she gazed over the brown landscape with splotches of snow.

"Hmm," was all that Riley could come up with in response.

"Well. He helped me see that being boxed in all the time isn't good for anyone's heart or spirit. Or their mind, for that matter," she said reflectively. "He encouraged me to take my heart out of the box stall and let it run free – like those antelope."

"Your father is a smart man, Shelby," Riley remarked. "Remind me to thank him for giving you that advice."

"So now my heart and spirit are out in the open," she explained. "And like those antelope, they are running full throttle, hopping and jumping and have a great time in the wide open spaces."

A noise from the bathroom startled Riley back to the present. He looked again at the clock. Yep. They were definitely going to be late. The song on the country music station had changed to the story of a husband who has taken his wife out for the evening and can hardly wait to get her home again.

The bathroom door swung open and Shelby stepped into the room as she announced, "Ready." Riley's gaze turned to drink in her slight form. He stared at her face where pale traces of the bruises remained, but she had expertly concealed them with makeup. His eyes traveled down her slender neck where he had discovered she loved to receive feather-light kisses. Then his gaze caught on the narrow shoulder strap of the dress and followed the edge of the fabric along its neckline to where it dropped just enough to be enticing. He stepped forward, and with his fingertips lightly traced the path his eyes had just taken. "I should have called and canceled," he said absently a second before he kissed his wife.

LOOK FOR
BREAKING FREE,
ANDREW AND ALLISON'S STORY,
COMING SOON!

Cadee Brystal's next novel is also set in Miller's Bend, where you've already met and grown to love the characters. Join Riley's brother, Andrew, and Shelby's friend, Allison, as they find the strength to trust each other and break free of their own personal past experiences.

EXCERPT

"Lucy ... had ... problems before we married," Andrew's voice had lost any trace of personal inflection or emotion. He didn't meet Allison's gaze, but looked beyond her, past her shoulder. Allison didn't know what he might be seeing behind her, but she was certain his focus was locked on something in the past. "I probably shouldn't have married her, but I thought it was the only way I could help Rori."

"That's sad," Allison spoke quietly.

"Yeah," he agreed as he pulled his focus back to Allison.

"You know what?" she said. "That's kind of noble – trying to protect Rori. But it's also kind of twisted."

"I'm not going to explain the whole thing now," he said in a businesslike manner. "I just don't want you thinking I'm pining over the loss of some great life-long love. It wasn't like that. I did what I had to for Rori. I guess I expected some loyalty and respect from Lucy in return and she stabbed me in the back."

"So you say," Allison spoke quietly. "I'm no expert on love, but I think you must have loved her on some level in order to feel as bitter as you do over the betrayal. She's got you more than a little messed up."

Andrew set his glass on the table as defensive instincts scrabbled to the forefront. "You think I'm messed up?" He started walking. Allison fell into step beside him.

"It wasn't an insult. Just an observation."

He snorted and kept walking.

"Look," she said as she laid a hand on Andrew's forearm, to get his attention. "Everyone has a past. We have to deal with it and then we break free from it." He didn't look at her. He couldn't risk exposing his insecurities, his demons. "If we don't," she continued earnestly, "then we are stuck wallowing in our history and we don't get to live our present and we deny ourselves positive futures."

"I'm not wallowing," he said defensively. "I just don't want to risk making the same mistakes again."

"That's understandable," she said as she raised her gaze to his. "Just don't assume that everyone is like Lucy."

Made in the USA
Middletown, DE
08 September 2015